Craig Saun

SCARECROW

&

THE MADNESS

Robert Essig

BLOOD BOUND BOOKS

ISBN 978-0-9845408-7-7

Artwork by Andrej Bartolovic

Printed in the United States of America

First Edition

Visit us on the web at:
www.bloodboundbooks.net

Anthologies Available from Blood Bound Books:

Rock 'N' Roll is Dead: Dark Tales Inspired by Music

Night Terrors: An Anthology of Horror

Unspeakable: A New Breed of Terror

D.O.A.: Extreme Horror Collection

Seasons in the Abyss: Flash Fiction Anthology

Steamy Screams: Erotic Horror Anthology

Novels & Novellas:

Monster Porn by KJ Moore

At the End of All Things by Stony Graves

Feeding Ambition by Lawrence Conquest

.

SCARECROW

Craig Saunders

Thursday

"Madge!"

"What?"

"Door!"

"I heard it. I'm doing breakfast!"

"I'm in the toilet, woman!"

Margaret swore under her breath and took the pan off the AGA cooker, the bacon still sizzling as she walked away. She wiped her hands on the tea towel, tossed it onto the worktop and headed along the hall to the front door.

She checked her hair in the full length mirror in the hallway. Grey, but tidy. Good enough.

There was a spot of fat on her dress. She thought about a quick change, but the ringing at the door wouldn't give up.

"Just a minute!" she called, pulling her hair back from her forehead with her palm. The strands fell back across her face as she pulled open the heavy door.

"Oh," she said, as she saw the policeman on her doorstep. He was smiling, but that didn't stop her asking, "Is something wrong?"

"No, ma'am," he said, keeping his smile in place. It came out as 'marm.' Policemen really did still speak like that in the rural heart of the fens.

"Can I help you?"

"I'm sorry, am I interrupting your breakfast?"

Well, yes, she thought, but responded, "Not at all."

He nodded. Took a breath. "It's just a courtesy call, really. We're stopping at all the homes in the area." He made a show of stepping back, taking in the view. "It's a nice house."

"Thank you," said Margaret, a trifle impatiently. She knew full well it was a nice house. It was a Georgian farmhouse; old enough to have space and style, but not old enough to be tumbling down around their ears.

The policeman coughed into his hand. When he took his hand away his beard was slightly askew, wiry ginger strands pointing this way and that.

Margaret wondered what the world was coming to. Police-men wearing beards indeed!

"Officer?"

"Ah. Yes. As I say, a courtesy. We thought we should let you know, there's a load of gypsies coming the weekend. A horse and pony show. The long weekend?"

"I know it's a long weekend, officer. Your point?" Margaret tried to smile as she said it. She was aware she was being brusque. She didn't like to be thought of as rude. She was, despite her best efforts, thought rude among the ladies of the parish council. Margaret simply was not a people person.

"Well, we thought we'd let you know. You know?"

"No, officer, I'm afraid I don't know. What about the gyp-sies?"

"They're in Mr. Davis' field."

"I know Mr. Davis. I'm sure who he lets in his field is of no concern of mine."

The policeman coughed again. This wasn't going how he had expected. "Erm, Mrs . . ."

"Rochette."

"Mrs Rochette, as I"m sure you are aware, gypsies are prone to stealing things, and can be quiet, ah, unsociable, shall we say?"

"Stealing away babies and suchlike?"

"Please, Mrs. Rochette. I'm just doing my job. I understand your point of view, but it's a fact. We're calling at all the houses in the area. I'd advise you to make sure your doors are locked, and the barns, too. You may wish to give them the benefit of the doubt, but we're letting you know for a reason. Thefts in the area rocket when-ever the gypsies come, and that's a fact, ma'am."

Margaret nodded. She deemed it the quickest way to get rid of the man. Her bacon would be ruined. She was more concerned about that than any gypsies.

"Well, thank you for the warning, officer. I'm sure I shall take it in the spirit intended."

The policeman wasn't sure how to take that. He tipped his hat and rubbed his face, seeming surprised to find his beard there.

"I'll leave it to you, ma'am."

"Is that all?"

"Yes. Good morning to you."

Margaret sniffed and looked out into the field past the policeman. The scarecrow was down again in the front field. She'd have to tell Bernie about that.

She closed the door.

The policeman shrugged and walked away. He'd tried. Some people just didn't want to listen to sense. Being politically correct was all well and good, he thought, but they hadn't called in reinforcements from three counties on a whim.

He turned up the gravel drive and gave one last look back at the house. It didn't look secure, but it wasn't his job to tell them that. He'd be a monkey's uncle if they didn't lose their best silver before the weekend was over.

* * *

Bernard came down the stairs hitching his trousers around his waist. He was a man with an ample waist and very little behind, hence his habit of pulling on his trousers. If he didn't, they were likely to fall down around his ankles at the most inopportune of moments.

"Who was it?" Bernard asked.

"The police."

"What? The police?"

"Yes, Bernie. The police."

"What?"

"The police, Bernie. Are you daft?"

"Hmm. Buggers. What did they want?"

"Apparently we're to batten down the hatches for the weekend. The gypsies are coming. If that young man had had his way we'd all be hiding in the cellar as if the Germans were coming."

"Gypsies, you say?"

"Yes, Bernie, gypsies."

"Hmm. Can't abide gypos." Bernard turned smartly on his heel after this pronouncement and walked out into the hall. Margaret sighed and followed him.

"Bernie?"

He was in the dining room, at the locked cabinet, fiddling with the lock. The lock and key were small, and Bernard's fingers large. Like sausages.

Margaret watched him with a frown on her face. Her arms

4

were crossed and her fingers tapped out a rhythm on her bicep, too. As if any one of the three signs of displeasure wasn't enough.

When Bernard turned around with the shotgun, a side-by-side Berretta twelve-gauge, she shook her head, just in case he didn't get the point.

"Where do you think you're going with that?"

"If the gypos are coming, I'm going to be ready. Thieving buggers."

She snatched the gun from him before he could load the shells he was fumbling with, and thrust it back in the cabinet. "Nobody is shooting anybody, you hear?"

"How are we supposed to protect ourselves if we haven't got a gun? I'm not young enough to be doing any fisticuffs, you know."

"Bernie, don't be an arse."

Bernard looked sufficiently chagrined, she thought. She held her hand out.

"Key," she demanded.

"Madge!"

"Key."

"Oh, blast it, woman. They'll be in here, raping you, you know? Stealing the cows and the silver."

"Key."

He puffed air through his red-veined nose but gave her the key.

He stalked out of the house. She put the key in her mother's blue vase.

Bloody fool, she thought. He'd probably shoot himself before he shot any gypsies, but she didn't trust him enough to take the chance.

Friday

The Volvo bounced and jostled its way along the dirty, pocked road. Bernard drove and Margaret watched the road, negotiating with Bernard as he negotiated with the road.

"One."

"Aw, come on, Madge."

"One," she firmly reiterated.

"Madge, seriously. I'm a grown man."

"Doctor Reed also says you're a grown man with a liver the size and texture of an elephant's testicle."

Bernard gaped at her.

"Oh, Bernard. Shut your mouth. You'll catch flies."

"That was two years ago, Madge."

"When you were turning yellow, I hasten to remind you, Bernie. One beer. That's your lot. If you can't promise me that, I won't let you go."

A lesser man might have argued the point. He might have said you can't stop me. But the simple fact was, Margaret could stop him. Bernard might not be the sharpest knife in the rack, but he knew when he was beaten. Every morning, he woke, opened his eyes, and thought, yep, I've lost this one, too.

It saved a lot of time in the long run.

"As you say, Margaret."

Something in his tone raised Margaret's hackles, but a huge pothole knocked her teeth shut.

"Damn it, Bernie! Watch where you're going! I damn near bit my tongue off."

Bernard kept his smile to himself.

They didn't talk until they got into town.

Bernard heaved himself out of the car, hitched his trousers, and nodded to his wife. He hadn't kissed her for . . . oh, damn near twenty years. Since their eldest was officially conceived, he believed.

"One," she said again, making the point with her finger, jabbing it at him over the roof of the car.

"Yes, dear," he said.

"Don't you . . . " she started, but he was already walking away.

She thought about chasing after him, but decided he'd stick to it. She turned and headed off to the market. It seemed busier than usual, with fewer stalls. She frowned, then remembered the gypsies. Apparently the market types didn't like gypsies, either.

More fool them, she thought. She looked at all the people milling around. She couldn't tell a gypsy just by looking. Must be one or two, she mused. Market was only busy in the summer with the tourists. Winter was knocking on the door. There were no tourists.

She smiled. Perhaps she'd meet a real life gypsy.

* * *

Bernard looked around to make sure she wasn't keeping tabs on him. He wouldn't put it past her.

"Same again?"

"Yes, I do believe I shall take another pint of Woodeford's finest, thank you very much." He laid a five pound note on the bar.

"Ah, Bernie, are you drunk?"

"Not at all," Bernard said, with a wink. "What leads to you to believe that?"

"I wonder," said the barman, with a wink for Bernard's companion.

"Because you talk like a Rupert when you've had too much to drink," said John, his drinking partner, neighbor, and fellow souse.

"I resent that implication," Bernard said, turned and took the two drinks from the bar, wiping the bottoms off on the Wherry's mat.

The barman put the change down.

"For you, my good man," Bernard told him.

"Thanks."

"Bernie, come and sit down, before you fall down." John shook his head. "Jesus, you've only had one. I dread to think what you'll be like after another."

"Blathered, one should hope," Bernard retorted.

"Come off it, acting the toff."

7

"Yeah, OK."

Bernard took a healthy gulp of his pint and wiped his lips. "Did you hear about the gypos?" he asked.

"Yeah. Bugger's are all over town. I saw one this morning, taking a piss up the front of the florists," John said, in the manner of a man imparting a great secret.

"Really?"

"Well, why would I lie?" said John, taking a healthy drag of his cigarette. You weren't supposed to smoke in pubs, but in the Red Lion you could pretty much do what you wanted as long as you hit the trough that passed for a toilet and didn't get too much sick on the tiles.

"I suppose. I heard they shit in the street. Like dogs."

"They don't pay poll tax, either."

"Buggers," said Bernard. The 's' was somewhat slurred.

"Used to be they stole children. Maybe they still do. You don't know, do you?"

"All the children go missing these days . . . well . . . there seems to be more gypsies. Makes sense." Bernard was half way through his second pint. Bad genes and a dodgy liver led him to believe that this was wisdom, damn it, *wisdom*.

"Thousands of 'em. Out in the field. They're tearing it up."

"Well, Davis knows what he's doing."

"You think so? Davis doesn't know what end he's talking out of, most of the time," said John, not quite as drunk as Bernard, but on his way.

Bernard pursed his lips and frowned as he thought about the statement. He let it pass. "Anyway, Margaret loves them."

"She what?"

"Oh, you know Margaret. She's all, you know, nignogs are people, too. She wanted me to take on some bloody Portuguese bugger in the summer, to help out. I said no, of course."

"Of course. You don't know, with them, do you?"

"No. Got nothing against foreigners, as such. You know. Like, well, Italians. You know where you are with them, sort of. Those funny new countries, though. You know," Bernard thought for a minute. Took another drink. "Well, you can't trust 'em."

"No, time was you knew where you stood with the foreigners. Used to just be the Germans, I suppose, back in the old days. I don't know. You've got all these, what are they called, Lithuanians?

You never used to have them."

Bernard nodded in agreement with this sage statement. "Another?"

Bernard nodded gratefully. "Thought you'd never ask."

John walked to the bar. Still steady.

The door swung in. Two young men, skinny jeans and tight tops, walked in. Bernard's first thought was: damn, the one on the left looks just like a cock.

He was a farmer, remember?

Because of the way his head popped on his neck, like he was pecking, tasting the air, taking in whiffs.

The one on the right had a little gold ring through his ear and a little thin thing just riding his lip. A bedraggled youngster trailed behind them. He looked about eight. He was sucking his thumb.

Could do with a good bloody wash, thought Bernard. But he wasn't drunk enough to say so.

Not yet.

John eyed the new arrivals warily as he set the pints down. "What'dya reckon? Gypos?"

A certain class of man doesn't know how to whisper. These two Fenland farmers were, by and large, among that class.

"Give us a pint," said the one with the thin moustache.

"Eh?" said the barman.

"Give us a feckin' pint, ya cunt."

"You calling me a cunt?" said the barman. He wasn't an east end barman, from the actual east end, or like you see in Eastenders. He didn't count himself a Mitchell. But that didn't mean he'd put up with people calling him a cunt.

"Aye. Ya's a cunt. Give us a pint."

"I'll have to ask you to leave."

"Jesus," said John.

"Here now," said Bernard, who was drunk enough, and a man. The thing about men is, even when they've got a beer gut, rheumy knees, and half a ton of years under their belt, they still think they're in their twenties. "You can't use that sort of language in here."

"Ya callin' us a cunt now?"

"Eh?" replied Bernard, confused.

"He's a fecker, Da," said the little boy, taking his thumb out of his mouth now that he felt he had something useful to say.

9

"Feckin' rite," said his Dad.

"Come now," said the barman, woefully out of his depth.

That was when the knife came out.

* * *

Margaret handed her money over at the fruit and vegetable stall. The lady behind the rows of vegetables—largely imported, Margaret was sad to see—fiddled in her little bum bag and passed Margaret a few coppers back with a forced smile.

Margaret didn't want to be rude, so she said 'thank you,' and tried to ignore the man shouting at another stall owner behind her.

It was difficult to maintain decorum when people were acting like that. The shouting man had filthy language, language she had never heard the like of before.

She wondered if she should intervene. The gypsy—not quite as swarthy and dusky as she had imagined—shouted something unintelligible and threw a coin at the stall owner. Then he took a large spanner from the display out front and brandished it at the owner when he tried to come around and deal with the man.

The man held his hands out, saying "OK, OK, take it. I don't want any trouble."

Margaret could see the man was shaking.

She couldn't understand all that the gypsy was saying, but she could tell there was a lot of language involved. Even the string of syllables was quite expressive.

The gypsy turned and bumped into her.

She felt some pressure on her handbag, and realized with sudden shock that he was trying to take her purse, which she'd left sitting on the top of her handbag so she could get to it easily.

"Oh, you bugger," she said. Her hands were full, so she did the only thing she could. She swung the bag of fruit and vegetables at his head. In the bag there was a melon, a head of cauliflower, and a few oranges.

The man with his hand of her purse didn't even notice them.

He did notice the cast iron kettle which was also in the bag. Margaret had picked it up for a song from the antiques stall.

He staggered back, blood suddenly flowing from a gash above his eye.

Margaret stepped back, too, from the sheer fury of the look

he gave her. It was murder, pure and simple. She'd never seen a look of murder in anyone's eyes, but there was no mistaking it.

She held up the bag with the kettle in it, like a talisman. She didn't think she'd get another swing in, but it was all she had to ward him off. She didn't have to hit him again, though. Just as the gypsy lunged toward Margaret a policeman walloped him on the head from behind.

The gypsy fell to the floor.

"Ma'am," said the policeman.

Her heart was fluttering madly in her chest. The policeman was calling his colleague to help him on a radio somehow stuck to his lapel.

"You ok, ma'am?"

"Yes . . . yes . . . I think so."

The two policemen picked up the unconscious man between them. The one on the left—too young, surely, to be a policeman— spoke into his walkie-talkie. A van with mesh over the windows pulled up almost immediately. The police bundled the man into the back, without too much care. In fact, without noticing the door swing ajar as soon as they'd shut it.

"Should I come with you? Give a statement, or something?"

"No, ma'am," said the one who'd done the hitting. "No point. He'll never see a cell. No point with the gypos."

"Oh," she said, surprised.

He looked like he wanted to say more, but just then his walkie-talkie squawked.

"Back-up, now! It's kicked off in the Red Lion, all available . . . fuck!"

The rest of the message trailed off as the man shouted at his colleague and they ran toward the Red Lion.

Oh. Shit.

Bernard.

Suddenly gypsies didn't seem so romantic anymore.

Margaret couldn't run. She had her hands full and wellies on. She made pretty good time though, across the road, up the street, following the sound of what could only be described as a ruckus.

The man in the back of the van shook his head to clear it. He opened the door and got out. Followed the woman down the road, where he ducked into the shadow of a shop door and watched her waddling progress.

The door tinged and a small lady piped up, "You can't stand there."

"Feck off," he said. He raised his shirt, showing the shop-keeper the handle of the knife.

The door tinged.

The man turned back to watching.

Behind him, the owner flipped the sign to 'closed' and locked the door.

* * *

"Come on, now, there's no need for that," said Bernard, still sitting.

Bernard was a farmer, in the Fens. He didn't know the first thing about bar fights. The last fight he'd had was at school, with Bicky Chapman. Buggered if he could remember his real name. Maybe it was Bicky. Stranger things have happened.

It was easy to tell Bernard had never been in a bar fight, be-cause he was still thinking about Bicky when the barman took the knife through his right hand, and *still sitting down*.

John, bless his heart, screamed like a girl and bolted for the door. The one without the knife, head bobbing like a cockerel, swung an arm at him. John took the punch on one meaty shoulder and made it to the door, where he began shouting.

"Help! Police! Fight! Knife!"

He covered all the bases. Then, because John had never been in a bar fight, either, he went back inside.

The barman was bleeding and holding the gypsy"s arm with his good hand, trying to fend the knife off.

Finally, Bernard decided to get up.

The other one, the one without a moustache, walked slowly toward Bernard.

Bernard, though slightly drunk, had one advantage: he out-weighed his adversary by roughly one hundred pounds.

On the negative side, that ten stone was mostly useless fat.

Bernard forgot about the fight going on with the barman and concentrated on the business at hand. And as he saw it, the business at hand largely consisted of not getting killed.

Despite never having been in a real fight, where people are actually trying to kill you rather than getting your flying saucers off you, he did the right thing, which is hit the other guy first with the biggest, hardest thing you can find.

The sway-backed old chair that had gamely held Bernard for so many years broke apart like deadwood, breaking the gypsy's arm. The gypsy, however, wasn't playing fair. In real life, Bernard reckoned that if you hit someone with a chair, they should have the good grace to give up.

The gypsy had other ideas. He kicked Bernard squarely between the legs.

Bernard doubled, grasped the man by the scruff of the neck and clung on for dear life.

Fortunately, the police took that moment to come charging in, grabbing everyone but the boy.

John was remonstrating quite strenuously.

The gypsies were kicking and punching whatever they could get hold of.

The barman was trying to staunch the flow of blood from his hand with a grubby beer mat.

The boy, finding himself unsupervised and forgotten, promptly ran and sank his yellow teeth deep into the flesh of Bernard's arm. Instinctively, Bernard swatted him with his free hand, like you would a bad dog.

"Aw, ya fecka. Ya broke ma 'ose."

"Good, you little shit. No more than you deserve."

The police had the brat's Dad on the floor. The one with the moustache was now unconscious by the bar, bleeding heavily from his head. One of the policemen, who was in fact a policewoman, was helping out with the barman's hand. No one was taking any notice whatsoever of the unconscious man on the floor.

"Ya fecka. Ay'm gonna get ya."

Bernard was aware his heart was dangerously high, fluttering about somewhere in the stratosphere. He reasoned out what the boy's Dad was saying.

"He bit me!"

"Ya shudna hit ma boy."

"Come on, you bastard," said one of the policemen, and dragged the Dad away. More policemen spilled in the door.

Bernard thought they looked disappointed that it was all over.

Margaret followed them in. When one of them tried to stop

her she stamped on his foot and rushed over to Bernard.

"Oh, Bernard. What have you done?"

"They just . . . " suddenly he felt very light-headed. He sat down on the nearest bench with a thump.

He sat with his back against the wall for a minute, until the stars floating in his vision went away. Policemen came up to him but he waved them away. Margaret fielded them, telling them his name, address . . . all the little things the police need to make violence fit on a sheet of paper.

"They just came in, started a fight," he told her, when he felt able to talk. "They stabbed Dave. In the hand. Fuck."

"Bernie, language!"

"Well, Madge, what do you expect?"

"Are you alright?"

"I'm fine. Bit too much excitement."

"Poor thing. It must have been terrifying."

"It was."

"Come on. Let's get out of here."

"The police will want statements, I expect."

Margaret sniffed. "I'm sure I don't care what they want. What you need is a good hot cup of tea at home."

And that was exactly what she told them when the police tried to stop them. The police could deal with violence all day long, but not the full force of Margaret's stony gaze.

"But . . . " said Bernard.

"At home, Bernie. Come along."

Bernie pushed himself to his feet. He swayed for a bit.

"How many did you have?"

Jesus. She was like a dog with a bone.

"Just the one. Just the one."

"Hmm," Margaret sniffed.

"Got a cold?"

She didn't reply. Didn't say a word, in fact, until they got to the car. It was very effective.

"I'm sorry," he said, as he drove out of the car park. "Maybe it was two."

Margaret nodded. It was as much as he was going to get.

As they took the road out of town, a battered old Vauxhall Nova pulled out behind them.

Bernard drove, though his head was pounding. He was almost sure he'd had a stroke, but people who'd had a stroke couldn't still drive, surely?

Either way, he didn't have a choice. Madge wouldn't drive. That was his job. She'd made that perfectly clear over the years. Even when the police had started clamping down on drunk driving, she had quite unreasonably expected him not to drink.

Nobody ever said she was a fair wife, he thought, sneaking glances at her as he drove. She was all hard angles. All the softness had been driven out of her.

He wondered if he could persuade her to put a nip of whiskey in his tea.

It was more of a daydream, really.

He drifted in his daydream. He'd had quite enough reality for one day.

The sheer speed of it! Life shouldn't be like that. It wasn't right. One minute they were having a pint, next minute there was blood and splinters.

Bernard still couldn't get his head round it. He wasn't stupid, but his mind worked in much the same way as his digestion. It was a stately process. It didn't have anything new-fangled like a metabolism to get in its way. His mind, as his gut, rumbled on towards their inevitable conclusions.

He was in this slow state of thought as he turned into to his pockmarked drive.

"Gonna get ya! Feckin' cunt!"

The shouting, along those lines, followed him from a battered Nova he hadn't noticed before.

"Oh, shit."

"Don't worry about it, Bernie. Probably just talk. Don't worry."

But Bernie did worry. He didn't have the stoic nature of a house brick, like Margaret, to fall back on.

Bernard watched his rear mirror all the way along the winding drive, but nobody followed him. When he pulled up beside the front door, gravel crunching as he braked, he noted even Margaret was worried. Her mouth was pulled in a tight line a man could cut himself on.

She told him not to call the police, barely moving her mouth

15

as she spoke.

"Don't bother, Bernie," she said. "They won't do anything."

She said this with such venom Bernard was suddenly more afraid of his wife than the gypsies. He trailed around the house after her as she locked and bolted all the windows. He thought it was supposed to make him feel better. But the very fact that Margaret thought they ought to lock the doors and windows didn't make him feel better. Not at all.

The day passed. He snuck a whiskey into his tea from his stash behind the cistern in the toilet.

They ate dinner. Chops, mash, squished cauliflower and cheese sauce.

Bernie tasted none of it.

He went to the toilet quite a lot.

"Nervous, dear," he told his wife.

Better put a stop to it, he thought. She's likely to smell it.

So he drank some milk.

Good for acid indigestion. Good for whiskey breath?

Who knows?

Finally, they went to bed.

He hadn't been as tired or drunk in a good long time.

Margaret smelled his breath. She let it go. When he was snoring deeply and soundly, she crept down the old stairs, avoiding the spots where the creak was worse, and into the hall.

She put her hand in the blue vase her mother had left her, took out the small key.

She was quiet when she unlocked and opened, then closed and locked the gun cabinet. It was steel. Steel has a habit of clanging if you're not careful.

Only when she had the gun cocked and loaded and stowed safely under their king sized bed did she close her eyes.

Saturday

Bernard felt the hand go over his mouth and tried to scream. A knife was glinting darkly in front of his eyes. Behind it there was a man. He wore a mask, but he flicked his eyes to the left and Bernard could see well enough to know he was expected to follow suit. He rolled his eyes to his right. Another man held a knife to his wife's throat. He held up a finger. Made a 'shh' gesture, then ran a finger across his own throat. Just in case Bernie was slow.

He was, but nobody was that slow.

The man holding a knife to Bernie's throat motioned for him to get up.

Bernie pleaded with his eyes. Please. Please don't hurt my wife. I'm begging you. Please.

One man led Bernard from the bedroom. The other stayed with his wife. Bernard began to cry. His tears were silent. Terror held his shout in his chest.

If he shouted, they would kill her for certain. He knew that without a doubt.

If he didn't scream, would they kill her anyway?

That he didn't know. Maybe they would. Oh God. Would they?

They were going to kill them both.

He knew, without them speaking, that these two men were gypsies. He didn't need to hear their dirty language or slurry syllables to understand this. Who else would do this to him? He'd never made an enemy in his life. Until the fight in the bar.

He made a lunge for the door. The man's hand came away from his mouth. He could have cried out, he could have screamed, but his breath caught. He couldn't make a sound. Then the man had hold of the neck of his pyjamas. He pulled him back with such force that the buttons popped on his top.

As if the point hadn't been made, the man pricked him with the knife as the hand slid back in place over Bernard's mouth.

This time he could cry out, but the hand muffled it.

17

Bernard felt blood trickle down his back. His pyjamas were suddenly dripping. He was sobbing against the hand over his mouth.

"Nay sound, ya fat bastard," the man said, whispering in his ear, "or ya bitch gets a new smile."

No sound. He got it.

Behind the hand – the hand smelled of animal flesh, horse, he thought, not cow – he bit down on his tongue until he tasted hot blood.

The man opened the door and pushed him out into the night.

There was a mild rain. The clouds were bright. The air prickled his flesh. He was goose-walked out into the field, the hand over his mouth, the knife in his back.

There was only one now. No one else. Now was his chance. If he didn't fight, they would die. They would both die.

Were they far enough? Would the man's accomplice be able to hear if he fought back now?

"He can hear fine," he said, as if reading Bernard's mind.

And then it was too late. They came from across the fields, out of the trees around the field, ten, then fifteen, then twenty. They looked similar. Family, thought Bernard, as far as coherent thought could take place. It was happening, but somewhere deep below, underneath the gibbering terror that was sitting on top, suffocating him.

"Ya shudna hit ma boy," said the man, and cracked Bernard across the back of the neck.

"Ya's a sorry cunt," he said.

Then they got to work.

Bernard came around half way through. There was nothing he could do. He could see, but he couldn't move his lips. There was pain when he tried to scream. They'd glued his lips together. He could see them, just, at the edge of his vision. Sometimes, they went away. When they came back they spat on him, cursed him, but they never kicked or hit him. They didn't have to.

Did they plan to leave him here? Leave him here to die?

He felt something rough stuffed up his sleeves, covering his hands. He tried to scream because he didn't know what it was, not because it was painful. The pain was constant already. Any more would just be lost in the landscape of pain that was his body.

Straw. They were covering his hands with straw. Finally he understood.

Then his view lurched. They heaved him from the floor. He lost sight of the sky for a time. They lifted him. It took more than one of them to do it.

Then they planted him in the dirt, in the middle of the field. The field he owned. The field he worked. Facing his house.

The boy's Dad filled his vision.

"Ma'be she's dead. Ma'be she's livin'. Ya's bin taught. Nobedy fecks wit' t'e Mulrones."

The gypsy patted Bernard's cheek. Said nothing more.

Then all Bernard could see was the field, his house, and the rain. He couldn't hear anything but the blood pounding in his head.

His arms, held straight out from his sides, began to go numb after a few hours.

Bernard didn't care by then. Even when his hands and arms and legs were numb, he could still feel the nails. Grinding, grinding, against his bones.

Dawn came. He remained. Still as a scarecrow.

* * *

Margaret woke as she did every morning: with a sigh. Another day. Something was amiss though. She rooted around in her mind, but it took no more than a second. No snoring, no weight.

And that was wrong. She woke her husband every morning. She was like clockwork. A rolex, maybe.

He, too, was like clockwork. The kind you got from Argos for £9.99.

"Bernie?"

She turned—she always slept turned away from her husband, he toward her—to find his side of the bed as she expected. There was a Bernie shaped dent in the soft mattress. A head sized dent in the down pillows. But no Bernie.

She pushed herself up and put on her slippers and dressing gown. She checked the bathroom—perhaps he had a hangover. She wouldn't be surprised. She checked the bottle behind the cistern and pursed her lips as she found it only half full. It had been nearer the top before yesterday.

If she didn't let him keep the bottle he'd only stash it somewhere else. At least this way she knew how much he was drinking and could water it down without him realizing. Still, half a bottle,

19

and she hadn't wanted to risk watering it too heavily . . .

She checked in the kitchen.

No sign of Bernie.

She knew him well enough to know that if he wasn't in the kitchen or the bathroom or the bedroom, he wasn't in the house.

She made herself a pot of coffee. He must be out in the field, or in the barn; unusual, especially after half a bottle of whiskey, but not unheard of.

She didn't think about their fright the day before until her second cup of coffee.

"Oh, fuck," she said.

Then she started to worry.

She didn't even put a coat on, but stepped out of the front door—it was locked, as she had left it—and headed over to the barn.

"Bernie!" she called, over and over, increasingly desperate.

She knew she was probably being foolish, but that instant of wrongness that had been there when she woke was growing stronger by the minute.

She poked her head in the barn. No one there.

Sometimes on a Saturday there would be help about, but not with autumn a memory and winter nipping at the door. There was plenty of work to do, but nothing they couldn't handle on their own. They weren't so old they couldn't run a small farm between the two of them.

"Oh, Bernie," she said out loud and was surprised at the depth of worry in her voice. That sense of wrongness was all around her.

She knew something had happened, but didn't know where to start.

She noticed Bernie had put the scarecrow back up. Perhaps he was out and about. Maybe with the shock of the fight in the pub... he was soft at heart, after all. He'd probably just gone for a walk out to the woods.

Probably.

The hell he had. Bernie had never gone for a walk for no reason in his life.

Some wives, some husbands, maybe they would have called around, called some friends, drank some coffee or something stronger. Gone about the business of waiting.

Wasting time.

Margaret wasn't that sort of wife.

She went back to the house and picked up the phone. She got the local police station after a short run around. Then she bullied them into sending an officer.

Then, that done, she sat down to wait, drinking coffee, tapping her nails against the kitchen table, staring out the window.

Worrying.

* * *

Margaret poured another coffee because she felt it was her duty. The policeman let her, because he was tired from a fight with his wife first thing in the morning, he was on an early shift, and he could do with an urn of coffee before he got back to the station. Plus, the coffee was really good.

"Run me through it again, ma'am."

Margaret sighed. She had many subtle ways of showing displeasure, but she deemed the policeman too stupid to pick up on anything less obvious.

"Officer, please. You're wasting time. The gypsies have taken my husband."

"Please, ma'am. One more time." Give me time to finish my coffee, he thought. Then he could get back to the station. Get some shut eye in the back cell. Not write a report.

He was good at not writing reports. It kept the crime figures down and made the force look good. They didn't want the real figures getting out.

They say the vast majority of crime is unreported. It is, but not by the good old taxpaying public. It's largely unreported by such fine upstanding members of the constabulary as P.C. Warburton, who had nothing whatsoever to do with bread, though not a week went by without one of his colleagues calling him crusty, or dough boy, or toast (when he came back from holiday in Alicante).

He couldn't even be in the same room as a dead body anymore. One more 'What'dya reckon? Brown bread, is he, Warburton?' and he'd quit. Fuck the pension.

The long and short of it was Mr. Rochette (Bernie) had gone missing in the night after a half a bottle of whiskey, a couple of pints in the pub, and a fight with some gypsies.

It was an every day story in the Fens. The gypsies liked

21

a fight, you could say that much for them. Bunch of psychos. He agreed with the dragon lady—as he'd come to think of Margaret—on that much.

But what the hell was he supposed to do?

He sighed and heaved himself up. Show willing, he supposed. Show willing, poke things with a pencil, mooch around the grounds. That sort of thing set their minds at ease.

Nine times out of ten the husband turned up after a day or two, having fallen down a ditch or into a twenty year old pole dancer.

He waved his mug hopefully as Dragon Lady finished her retelling.

Margaret took his mug and put it in the sink.

"Well," said P.C. Warburton, not one to flog a dead horse, "Shall we have a sniff about, see if we can find a clue?"

People liked the idea of clues.

"I'm sure you could do with one," said Margaret.

"Quite so, ma'am," he said, not really listening. "Door locked, was it?"

"Yes. I've told you that twice." Margaret paused. "Three times, now. Would you like me to tell you again? So you can write it in your little book?"

Warburton didn't want to get his book out again, not with Dragon Lady standing beside him. He didn't think she'd appreciate the doodles of large breasts and buttocks.

"No need, ma'am. Photographic memory, see?"

"Really? For what? Tits and arse?"

Shit.

"Don't bother. I shall be calling your superiors shortly. Here is the front door. See? Unlocked. I shall be sure to lock it again once you are on the other side of it. Good day, Mr. Warburton."

"P.C. ma'am."

"How do the young people put it? Whatever. Yes, I believe that is the expression."

Then P.C. Warburton was on the gravel drive. Suddenly he didn't want to go back to the station house. Not a little bit. He was going to get a right bollocking.

He was, in fact, brown bread.

* * *

22

Margaret fumed for a long time. How on earth was it fair that they paid so much more council tax and got so much less out of it?

There were plenty of jobs that needed doing around the house, around the farm. On a farm, there is always something that needs doing.

But she just couldn't face it. She couldn't stomach looking at the dumb cow's face. It would only remind her of Bernie.

Come on, come on. Think.

There was no way anybody could break into the house. The doors were all locked, the keys were where she usually put them.

Maybe there was a noise, Bernard got up, went to investigate...no, Bernie wasn't like that. He would have woken her and sent her down.

Maybe they were outside, he woke in the night to go to the toilet, saw them from the window . . . called down? Chased them off?

No. Ridiculous.

Maybe he'd taken his keys, gone out, locked the door behind him . . . but where? He hadn't taken the car.

Don't be silly, Margaret, she said to herself. They took him. You know it. Stop beating about the bush. Deal with it. That's what you do.

Where would they take him?

Would they have killed him?

Don't think like that. Don't think it.

But she couldn't get the idea out of her head.

There were some things she did know. Her husband was missing. The gypsies had something to do with it. Anything else didn't matter. How they did it, irrelevant. What they wanted, irrelevant. The sheer anger and hatred she'd seen in the men in the barroom brawl, irrelevant.

What did she want?

Her husband back. He wasn't perfect, not by a long shot. But he was hers.

Maybe they'd killed him?

Damn it, woman! Stop thinking like that.

Do something about it.

She got her car keys from the little drawer beside the door and locked the front door on her way out. She fiddled with the car seat, the mirror, did all the things she saw Bernard do. She'd never driven in her life, but, she reasoned, if Bernard could do it, how hard could it be?

She lurched along the potholed road. By the time she reached the public road, she was smooth, straight, and doing sixty.

On the way to Davis' field.

* * *

Bernie came around and screamed. He didn't make a sound. That was bad, but not the worst. The worst thing was that the weight of his head falling down against his chest had cut off his air. He could have died.

The pain in his legs, in his arms, was terrible, terrifying, but it was background. The circulation had cut off. There was nothing he could do about that. But he'd torn some skin from his lips when he'd tried to scream and now he could taste the blood. The taste of fresh blood somehow woke him up in a way that the panic and pain could not.

When you taste blood, you know it's real.

Then he screamed some more as a strong wind made his makeshift cross sway and the nails in his forearms and his shins grated against the bone. Blood started to flow afresh and he sobbed, unsatisfying, muffled sobs.

He was beyond terrified. He was way over into despair. Resignation was the next town over, but he wasn't quite there yet.

The hood had shifted so that all he could see was a stretch of tilled earth and the outer curve of his gut, his spiteful gut, which was pulling him down.

It wouldn't be the blood, or the nails, which killed him. It would he his great fat gut, pulling his chest forward, pulling his shoulders back, crushing his ribs, exhausting him, until his head fell again, fell against his chest . . .

Then, he would stop breathing. And he would never know. Never know if she was alive or dead.

What a terrible way to go. To die, never knowing if the one woman you ever loved made it through, or if she died along with you.

Bernard didn't believe in heaven. He didn't believe they'd meet again. He believed in dirt, and worms, and an afterlife as compost.

24

He didn't want to die not knowing. He didn't want to die. Full stop.

So what can you do about it?

Got to get moving, Bernie. Got to get moving.

Get to the house.

And yet, he thought, with as much sarcasm as he could manage, you've been planted in a field and you're nailed to a cross and you can't see. If you do somehow get out of the ground, and fall on your face, you'll be just as dead, because believe me when I say you'll never get up again. Not in this life. The next thing you know, you'll be part of the great cycle of life. You know, the one you talk about when you're drunk and the conversation in the pub turns to God and things of that ilk?

So, Bernie?

Bernie had started talking to himself at some point while he was thinking. He realized he didn't like that voice, but that voice was company. That voice was sanity. Because the other voice, the one he could hear whispering in the background, quiet so far, but with an option on shouting at some point in the very near future, that voice, that voice . . .

Sanity said to him, you don't need to worry about that.

Bernie thought, what do I need to worry about?

Getting out of the ground. Getting moving.

And Bernie added, and not falling down.

For God's sake, don't fall down.

* * *

Margaret pulled up on the road. She might have learned to drive, but she didn't have the first idea how to park. She could, of course, if she set her mind to it. She just didn't want to learn, and she didn't have the time or the inclination.

She slammed the door and locked it. She'd never trust gypsies again. And she was, as she was sure she'd heard on some television programme or other, in their manor.

As far as gypsies had a manor.

She stomped up the road, across the mud, stepping around or over or through manure and dog's doings without a thought, to the nearest caravan.

In the center of the field was a clear area, with some tethered horses (my God, she thought, is that a *chain* round that horse's neck?) and some dogs, healthy and mangy alike, sharing the space. All around the center were caravans, little dirty ones, clean ones, old ones, new ones. Cars in similar states of repair, from the new to the old. Vans, campers, horse boxes, a trap as in a God damned pony and trap, and people.

So many people.

And Margaret was very, very, very aware that despite all of the people doing various people things, she wasn't one of them.

She was different people. She hadn't understood, not really. Not until now. She was people, alright, but she was *her* kind of people. These were *their* kind of people.

But really, that didn't matter. Not one little bit. Because somewhere, someone, one of these people, knew what had happened to her husband. She was absolutely sure of it.

She became even more sure when she saw the look on the face of a man tugging a dog on a length of rope, eyeing her. She remembered a look of murder, and the face and the memory slid across each other until there was an almost audible click within Margaret's mind.

"You!"

You'd think he'd have the decency to run away, she thought. She could do with the exercise. But no, he just stood there, watching her approach.

Someone grabbed her arm and she was so het up she swung an arm at him.

"Easy, lass. Ya got bizniz wit' t'e Mulrones?"

The man looked kindly at her. A little sadly.

"If that's them, then yes," she said curtly, snatching her arm free.

"Ya had best turn around, t'en. Best get gone."

She shook her head.

"I can't. My husband . . . "

She didn't need to say more.

"Sorry ay am, te hear t'at." He shook his head and walked away. She turned to watch him go. What did he mean?

Oh, bastard, she thought as she turned around. If he hadn't stopped her, she could have got the man alone. Now it was too late. Another couple of men walked up to him – brothers? Now she was stomping toward three men. They were joined by more. They just

26

kept coming.

It seemed the Mulrones were legion.

She didn't bother counting. There were enough. Suddenly she thought that coming here had been a bad idea. One of her worst.

Hmm. A very bad idea indeed.

But that wouldn't stop a woman like Margaret.

"You there! What have you done with my husband?"

"Lost him, have ya?"

"You know full well what I'm talking about! And speak properly, damn it!"

"Get ya gone!" yelled a woman, young, wearing a short top that showed a map of stretch marks across a loose belly. The girl – she could be no more than twenty – spat on the ground.

"Not until you tell me what you've done with him. You… you…pikeys!"

They laughed at that. One of them stepped forward, reached out to push her. Just as the hand fell on her another voice shouted out.

"Hoy! Stop t'ar! Wot ya's doin' ta t'ar lady?"

A little old woman was stalking toward the group of them. Physically, she was incapable of stalking. She was bent almost double. Her joints were like tree knots. The old woman's stalking days were done, but she was stalking, nonetheless.

It was in the set of her face, her stony eyes. Margaret could feel her will from ten feet away, and she was damn grateful for the interruption.

She had an idea things were about to go seriously wrong. The kind of wrong, she thought, where nobody but those involved knew just how wrong things went, because nobody else would ever see or hear from her again.

She wished she'd just waited for Bernie to turn up.

But then she knew things had gone way beyond that. These people had hurt him. Maybe done something worse.

She didn't want to think about that. But as frightened as she was, she wouldn't let it go. He was her husband.

"Wot ya doin' here, lady?"

"They did something to my husband! I know they did. They took him. Maybe hurt him. Did you hurt him, you bastards?!"

"Hoy, ma, she's callin' us bastards!"

"Ya's are, Rob. Now, wot did ya's do?"

27

There was a string of something Margaret didn't understand, then the one the old woman had called Rob said, "But he hit ma bo'!"

"Ma'be. Ma'be. But ya no shuda done t'ar. Ya's a bad boy, Rob."

"Ya can no say it's no fair, ma," said Rob. The others in the group were nodding. Now Margaret was looking, she could see similarities between some of them. A family. God help her. She was facing down a family of them. Not a family like hers. This was the kind of family people make movies about. The kind of movie where the hero get stranded in the wilderness and ends up being eaten.

If it hadn't have been for the mother (Grandmother? She dreaded to think how long the old lady had been breeding for, if this was her brood) she would be in trouble. Serious trouble.

In fact, she might already be at that point. Her life was, quite literally, in the old woman's hands.

The old lady seemed to think. Margaret didn't think . . . no, she knew…she wouldn't get a damn thing from the kids, cousins, whatever they were. She had one chance. One chance only.

The old woman bit her wrinkled lip with one remaining yellowed tooth.

Rob said, "Fair's fair, ma."

She held up a hand to silence him. Margaret didn't think anyone but this one bent old lady could have done that to him, or any of the others. She was like some kind of juggler. Her children were balls of fire. Margaret was willing to bet this old woman had never been burned.

"Lady," she said. "Ya go on. Leave now. He be on t'a farm. Ya find him, ya keep him. Ya no come back here. Get gone."

She stared at Margaret. Margaret stared right back.

Margaret had never met her match before in a staring contest, but she knew she wasn't going to win. She didn't waste any more time.

She nodded curtly. She was fuming. But she was unhurt, she knew Bernard was alive, and…well? She didn't know that, but she wasn't stupid. It was the best she was going to get. It would have to be enough for now.

As she turned on her heel the old woman descended back into that weird language. Not shouting, but cutting and whipping just the same, she had no doubt.

Someone shouted that they would get her. Rob. She knew his voice, now. That voice made her blood run cold. She was scared. The hairs on her arms stood straight out, some primal response to her fear.

She daren't turn back. She daren't look over her shoulder.

There was a crack. Margaret had kids herself, long grown now, but not so long grown she didn't remember the sound a good solid clip round the ear made.

The last thing she heard was the old woman.

"Ya's'll get no one, ya git."

It was just high jinx to them. Spirited children, playing. But children could bite, and kick, and pinch, and punch. Children could be mean and dangerous.

They were different people. If her kind of people did their kind of playing they would be in jail. She dreaded to think what their kind of playing was. She didn't want to think about it. She just wanted to get home, find Bernard, and for this all to be over and done with.

She didn't look back. She got in the car. Drove. Shaky, then smooth, then fast.

Going home.

Hold on, Bernie, she thought. Oh God, Bernie, wherever you are, whatever they've done, you just hold on.

* * *

If he threw himself forward, Bernard thought perhaps he could snap the wood off, break it out of the ground. Then what? Fall on his face, for certain.

After that . . . wriggle? What, a quarter of a mile? Nailed to a piece of wood?

Bugger that.

Your weigh might tear the nails out if you try to move.

That voice. That morning, the voice had been just a whisper. But it was getting louder as the day went on.

It was making more sense.

Yes, imagine the pain. The pain would be tremendous. And the blood . . . the blood would pour. You might lose consciousness. You could die.

That was the voice Bernie liked. That voice was looking out

29

for him.

No, it's not. Listen to that and you'll die. Crucified. Sure, made to look like a scarecrow, but really, you'll be crucified. You'll wither. The bugs will eat your flesh. A year from now, maybe less, maybe more, when the flesh has all gone to dust, your bones will fall free of this cross and you"ll still be dead.

Shut up! Shut up!

Then move, you fucker. Move.

Except fucker didn't sound quite like that. It sounded more like 'fecka,' and that sent shivers down Bernard's spine.

The voice was frightening him.

Then both voices, good and bad, were lost to him, because there was sudden, blinding agony from his legs, legs he thought long dead to all feeling.

But they felt this. Oh, yes, Jesus, they felt this.

His weight, pulling him down, finally tore something loose. The nails, through his flesh, into the wood, which had chipped but not pierced the bone on either side, tore long gaping holes in his calves. His arms held, and the weight on his shoulder increased, then decreased, as his feet slid slowly, oh, so slowly down the wooded post to the ground, where, mercifully, they came to rest.

Bernard's head shook from side to side. Unable to scream, he shook and trembled and cried in his agony. The sudden movement sent the blood rushing back to his feet and then the pins and needles started.

And it was far, far worse.

Bernard had never known such pain existed.

He would have gone utterly mad, perhaps beyond redemption, if it hadn't been for the sound of the car, crunching over the distant, potholed drive. He could see the house now, since shaking his head. The sackcloth, with two holes for eyes, had shifted.

For the first time he registered that the Volvo was not on the drive. Then the car came into view.

Please, please, he thought, hope and fear driving the pain from his mind for precious seconds.

Margaret got out of the car.

Throw yourself forward! She'll see you!

He leaned, ready to do just that, but at the last instant he registered the lilt, the 'ya' that should have been 'you,' and braced himself on feet that were alive again, with pain, yes, but alive.

He wouldn't do that. Couldn't listen to that *voice*. That wasn't the way.

He flexed his toes until he thought he could feel, distantly, earth underfoot. That was the way. Patient.

He could also feel wetness, thick on his legs and ankles, and that wasn't so good. He thought that was blood, and lots of it.

He got the idea that maybe patience was good, but not too much patience, because even fat men only bleed so long, and then...

Ya cunt, said the voice.

But he didn't listen, and the voice faded, back to a whisper. A murmur, and hint.

Bernard's head sagged forward, and then there were no more voices, just black sleep.

* * *

Margaret put the key in the lock, put her shoulder into the old warped door and pushed her way into the house.

The house felt cold to her. A cold made somehow deeper by the house's emptiness. The lingering smell of coffee came from the kitchen, but it was a stale smell that made her gag.

Stop being such a chit, she chided herself. She took big gulps of air, trying to settle herself. That just made things worse. Stars danced across her vision. She put her hands on her knees and bent forward to make the stars go away and vomited on her shoes.

"Oh, Madge," she said, as the tears came.

She stayed that way, hands on her knees, staring at her small pancake of watery vomit. Her tears dripped, splashing into the sick. The sight made her want to throw it all up, all her fear, all her anger, but she pushed herself straight.

"Enough."

She stepped around the mess, walked down the hall and took out the mop and bucket. Ran some water. Squirted in the cleaner.

When she was done, the slate glistened.

Then, she emptied the bucket. Rinsed it out in the old sink at the back of the house, put everything away.

Cleaning up wasn't wasting time. A woman could think and mop. A man, well, he would probably struggle to concentrate on more than two things at once. Women have different skills though. Like finding things.

31

For instance, Bernard would say to her, head in the pantry, "Madge, we're out of HP."

Margaret would move a jar of pickle, maybe gherkins, maybe Branston, and lo, "Look, would you? What do you call that?"

Bernard would look sheepish for a while, take the HP sauce and lather his sausages, his thick hands bashing the base of the bottle.

She started upstairs. She didn't try to think of likely places a man Bernard's size could be stashed. She started at the beginning. She intended to search everywhere, until she found him. Ticking off a mental list she had made while she had been mopping up her mess.

Their bedroom. Unlikely. Really unlikely. But the point of searching for things is that if you don't know where something is, the chances are it's not where you'd think.

Under the bed. In the closet. Behind the shower curtain in the en suite they had put in five years ago.

A spot of black mould on the grout, down the bottom where the water had a habit of pooling if it wasn't wiped after a shower, and Bernard never wiped.

She made a note to deal with that.

Three spare bedrooms. Nothing. The last, the smallest, they used mostly for storage. There was a chest in there, a big old antique thing. Bernard was too big to fit in there, but she checked anyway.

She knew why she checked, but she didn't let herself think about what would have to be done to a man to fit him in that kind of space.

Nothing.

She paused at the top of the stairs. They'd have had to bind Bernard – if that was all they had done to him—gag him, or she'd have heard him calling out. All done so quietly that she hadn't woken. Upstairs was extremely unlikely. She'd checked everywhere, hadn't she?

All the wardrobes—each more than big enough to fit a man in, even one of Bernard's girth. The wardrobes were all antiques. Nearly as old as the house, some of them.

The thing with people with money is this: they spend less, because the things they do buy *last forever*.

Bernard's parents had run this farm before them, and their parents before them. And not one of them had ever had to buy any furniture, because the furniture in the house was nigh on immortal.

Thinking about upstairs, Margaret also thought about the furniture, which pieces would be large enough to hide a large man, and—

The boot of the car

The downstairs toilet

The back porch

Their industrial-sized washing machine (unlikely, but if they'd broken his arms and legs . . . stop!)

The bottom of the Welsh dresser

The sideboard

The base of the couch in the living room

In the alcove behind the mahogany shelves

Up the chimney in the Inglenook

So on.

She went on, checking everywhere she could think of. Methodical. Cold. Not panicking.

She searched, until she could search no more without a cup of coffee and something to eat. She ate toast and pushed down her fear. No time for that. Food was essential. She couldn't carry on if she didn't eat, but she didn't need to waste time on fear.

"Shit," she said, half way through her second piece of toast. "The bloody attic, fool woman."

She finished her toast first.

* * *

When Bernard drifted back into consciousness his mind couldn't get started. Thoughts skirted his grasp, slapping and pinching, laughing as they ran off.

Come back, you bastards, he tried to say. He realized he couldn't open his mouth. Couldn't move his legs. There was something holding his arms out straight. Pinching, but distant. His shoulders were on fire.

His legs . . . there was something wrong with his legs.

He couldn't see. Gummy eyes maybe. A heavy night.

He tried to move his arm to rub the sleep from his eyes, but the bloody thing had gone dead.

Margaret?

Pins and needles in his foot. He kicked out, then it hit.

His right leg tore free, leaving a chunk of leg behind between

33

the nail and the post. He screamed and screamed and nobody could hear him. Even though his legs were dead, there was a core, deep inside, that could still feel. A part of him that knew he had torn a good sized piece of his leg off.

Now you'll bleed to death.

Now ya'll bleed ta deat'

Oh no.

Fuck off! Leave me alone!

But it kept on. A taunting, evil bastard of a voice. On and on, until he couldn't hear the voice of sanity anymore. The gypsy voice, the pikey voice, had taken it and put it in chains, in a deep dark box, just as dark as it was for Bernard.

But for a whisper.

One leg's free, Bernard, it said.

The hard part's done, it said.

Feckin' shut ya mouth

But he concentrated, concentrated so hard, until he could hear that voice, the good voice, telling him what to do. How to do it. How not to fall on his face.

His arms weren't shifting, but he had a foot free.

Work some life into it, Bernard. It'll hurt like a bitch.

Dyin's easy, fecka. Give up, die

No. Dying's easy, sure. This way'll hurt. But you'll live, Bernard. You'll live.

The pain was immense. The blood was pouring. That was a problem. A big problem. So was the weakness, the bright lights drifting across his vision, even though he knew it was full dark beyond the sack.

But dying was easy.

Yes, but that wasn't his voice. That was them.

The voice kept on. Bernard shut it out. Swore at it. It didn't go away, but he was getting angry. Angry was good.

Because now he had his free leg, his right leg, planted, firm, in the dirt. He had no leverage to tear his left leg free, but he couldn't face that, anyway. He just couldn't.

But that didn't matter, because he didn't want to do that. Even if he somehow tore both legs free, it wouldn't help, because then he really would fall. His arms would come free, but there would be massive holes, pouring blood. He'd bleed to death in the dirt, face down, not too long after he passed out from the pain.

He mustn't fall.

His right leg planted, he leaned forward. Let his weight pull the plank. The nails in his arms and his left leg pulled tight. Blood started to pour again, but not in floods.

Immense pain. A whole country of pain. A continent. A world.

And a snap. The most beautiful sound he'd heard in all his life. It drove away the pain.

There was a moment of panic as he tottered on a torn leg and dizziness washed over him, but then he was straightening, one free leg, one nailed leg, using the post now to hold him up.

Good, Bernard. Now for the hard part

Ya's'll bleed ta deat' b'fore ya get home

Fuck off, you bastard, said Bernard, and began to move.

Sunday

He wasn't on the property. There was nowhere he could be. Margaret had searched the attic, the barn, the hayloft, the garage, the car, the cab of their old rusty tractor, the bed of the trailer…

She was getting tired. She looked at the grandfather clock in the hall. Just standing there. Swaying. Two o'clock. Two o'clock in the morning.

"Bernie, I'm sorry," she said. She wondered if he was somewhere he could hear her. Maybe stuffed into a wall.

Think straight, woman, she said in her sternest voice, the one she used only for herself.

She couldn't go on. She wasn't thinking anymore, she was just roaming from room to room. Like some ditzy, giggling girl.

"Come on, Madge," she said. "That's what he'd say. Come on, Madge. Get your thinking cap on.

"I'm sorry, Bernie. I need a coffee if I'm going to keep going. Just hold on. I'm coming."

She walked into the kitchen, the floor squeaking, and did the little things that people do when terrible things happen. She tapped the filter on the side of the bin, emptying the coffee grinds. Measured out two mugs of water, two desert spoons of coffee, flicked the switch, and listened to the steady gurgle of the water working its way through the coffee, into the pot.

She paced. The floor squeaked again. It took a while to register. She was dog tired.

"You stupid cow!" she cried and fell to her knees, beside the cellar door.

She pulled on the ring set into the boards on the floor, yanked the door open. It was the old cellar. It had flooded years back and the smell of damp and rot blasted up.

"Hold on, Bernie!" she called down into the wet darkness. "I'm coming!"

She was so sure that was where he was. She hadn't thought of it because they never used it. It would cost a fortune to fix it up.

She ran back out into the hall, to the cabinet where she put the flashlight after searching the barn.

At the top of the cellar, she paused, but just for a second. The stairs down were wooden. Years of damp. Years of rot. Would they hold her?

She couldn't worry about that now. She shone the light into the dark, searching around, but the cellar was an L-shaped room. She couldn't see round the corner. If Bernie was round that side, unconscious (hurt?) he might not hear her. She had to go down.

She stepped carefully, near the edges of the risers, not in the center. The stairs groaned ominously as they took her weight. They complained, but they held.

"Bernie?" she called, as she reached the bottom. "Bernie?"

No sound. No breathing.

She peered round the corner, gaze glued to the small circle illuminated by the flashlight. He wasn't there. She let out the breath she'd been holding.

A crash came from above. Then another.

They'd come back!

Shit, she thought. She realized she'd left the shotgun under the bed. The sound of breaking glass had come from downstairs. They were in the house.

She had to get past them to get the shotgun.

She broke into a run. Took the stairs with her full weight. The first five steps held just fine. The sixth snapped clean through with a terrifying sound louder even than the breaking glass.

* * *

"Ay'nuff," said Rob, ruffling his son's hair.

"Aw, Da'."

Rob shook his head.

The boy dropped the stones he'd been holding, but didn't complain further. He followed Rob back to the battered old van they were driving.

They didn't even bother to look for the scarecrow. The night was pitch black. They wouldn't have seen it, and anyway, that was done. The man had been taught.

The woman, too.

She had been taught.

Vengeance, cold and brutal, had blown itself out. Rob and his boy drove back to Davis' field, where they would pack up. By first light, they would be gone. A whirlwind, spent.

In the dark, the scarecrow moved closer. Paused. Swayed. Closer.

A cold rain started to fall. The wind picked at the straw. The sheet covering it fluttered and flapped, stuck, picked up again.

Muffled sounds came from the scarecrow. Grunts. Cries. No words. Just pain, determination, and something that made the blood run cold.

Muttering, purely nasal. But even without words, you could tell the scarecrow was arguing with itself.

Sanity and insanity, at war.

* * *

Margaret sat up and rubbed her head. She'd knocked herself a good one on the way down. She pushed herself to her feet, noticed her hand wouldn't work properly and hurt like hell.

"Well, that's a bastard," she said, with very little passion, looking at her broken wrist. She flapped her hand around to make sure. There wasn't much pain. Perhaps the nerves were torn. She just couldn't seem to care.

Blood ran into her eye. She wiped it away with her free hand. She tried to raise some emotion. She was sure there was some reason she was at the bottom of the old cellar, but for the life of her she couldn't think of it.

But either way, she wasn't banged up enough to think sitting around down here was a good idea.

She eyed the steps warily. There was something about those steps...

Three of them seemed to be missing.

"Bernie?" she called. He'd help her. All she needed was a ladder. And maybe an ambulance. She'd call them when she got to the kitchen. The coffee was on. The smell made her mouth water.

"Bernie?"

More urgent this time. What if he was in the field?

Margaret was beginning to worry. If he was in the field, she might be stuck in here all day.

But there was a knocking sound from somewhere above.

38

Somewhere distant. Upstairs?

She shouted louder. As loud as she could manage.

Dun Dun Dun Dun...

What was that?

"Bernie!"

He's not coming.

Of course he is. He's just not . . .

No . . .

Hang on . . .

He's not coming.

Suddenly she had a blinding headache and she remembered why Bernie wouldn't come. She was searching for *him*.

Oh shit.

Now I'm really in trouble.

She remembered the gypsies.

Then the past day came screaming back at her, from waking (no Bernie) to the police (Warburton, right?) to searching, the stairs, the glass breaking . . .

Oh, my God, she thought. They're in the house and I'm stuck in the cellar.

And I've just been letting them know where I am.

She stared up at the square of light above her, her blood cold, her limbs frozen. Terror had seized her strength.

She took her broken wrist and thumped it, hard on the side of the stairs. She had to bite back the scream but it did the trick. She was moving again.

She wasn't stuck. She wasn't some stupid girl. She used her common sense.

Margaret took the bottom three stairs carefully, then reached up and took hold of the next unbroken riser with her good hand. There were waves of pain coming from her wrist, her hand. Her whole arm was throbbing, but she needed it. Not the hand. The pain.

She placed one foot on the side runner, still wood, and perhaps rotted, but now her weight was along the narrow part, with the whole width of the wood supporting her weight, rather than her weight being on the width with only the narrowness of the plank to support her. Using her hand to guide her, she shuffled her feet along the edges of the stairs, until her hand finally clasped the floor above.

When she came out, she flopped onto the floor and drew in great heaving breaths. She could have happily laid there for a week, but the banging from upstairs was suddenly joined by another, more insistent banging.

At the backdoor.

The French windows.

They were trying to break the French windows. The realization hit her. There was more than one. It might be all of them. The whole of the Mulrone clan. Come to finish it.

Well, fuck them.

She pushed herself up, put her head down, and ran for her bedroom.

For the shotgun under the bed.

* * *

Bernie!

Bernie!

The voice sounded familiar. So familiar. But he couldn't think straight. The voices were drowning out all sounds, all thoughts. The pain, too, was gone . . . away. His arms, his legs . . .

They were like Spain. The pain had emigrated.

Probably frightened of the gypsies. People were frightened of them. He knew that. Frightened of the Polish, the Portuguese, the Croatians, the Indians, the French, goddamn it. People were afraid of the French.

Bernie wasn't afraid of any of them. He had a gypsy friend. He was a good friend. Best friend he ever had. The man made sense. He'd got him moving. He knew Bernie couldn't do the front door. Of course he couldn't. His arms were in Spain. You can't do complicated doors when your limbs have emigrated.

Aye, now swing, like t'at, t'at's it, swing, the voice, the gypsy, said.

Another voice said, Bernie, you know you're going insane, don't you? Don't you? Bernie?

But Bernie didn't like that voice so much right now. That voice kept telling him off. He wasn't a little boy. He was a man.

T'at's rite. Ya's a man.

Damn right.

His hand went through the glass. He twisted, like his gypsy friend told him to. Took the weight on his right leg. Shuffled . . . like so . . . hand through the gap . . . just a little further . . . click.

40

Now turn it, said another voice. Bernie wasn't sure who it was. He pushed and the door popped open.

Remember why you're here? Remember Madge.

That voice. That thrice buggered voice. What did it think? Did it think Bernie was stupid?

Of course not.

Ah, but ay do, ay do.

Get out. I'll do it. I'll get her. I'll get Madge. I know why I'm here. She's my wife, you fuck. Don't patronize me.

He could see very little, but he remembered his own house well enough, thank you. He shuffled, round the kitchen table.

In a good world, perhaps Bernie would have gone round the side with the trapdoor open and waiting.

In a good world.

He reached the foot of the stairs.

Then there was thunder, and he screamed.

His lips tore free at last and he swallowed the blood and cried out for his wife.

"Madge! Madge! I've come to get you!"

* * *

Margaret ran straight into the bedroom, snatched the gun from where it hid under the bed.

She took some shells and put them into her pockets.

If they were all here she wouldn't die because she did something as stupid as running out of shells.

A crash came from the kitchen. They'd broken the French doors. But more immediate was the banging coming from the spare bedroom.

She checked the load, not so easy one handed, then snapped the gun closed. There were no hammers on the Beretta, just a switch to choose which barrel to fire.

She rushed into the bedroom and fired at the sound.

The rocking chair exploded, splinters flying everywhere.

She was losing it.

Her ears rang, but she could still hear footsteps at the base of the stairs.

They were really coming this time.

She took a deep breath. Then she walked along the hall, toward the stairs. She'd hold them here. The house was built to last. So was she. She wouldn't let them beat her.

They'd taken her Bernie. She'd take them.

She broke the gun, spat out the spent shell, slammed another in, turned the corner.

There was some terrible thing, some sick, sad joke, standing at the foot of the stairs.

"Ay've come ta g'rt ya!" it cried.

"Like fuck you have," she said, and gave the pikey bastard both barrels.

The scarecrow slumped to the floor and reality sank back in.

"He be on t'a farm. Ya find him, ya keep him."

An old woman. A gypsy.

The scarecrow, standing in the field again.

Margaret dropped the gun. It tumbled, end over end, to the foot of the stairs, where it came to rest on her husband's ruined chest.

She took the stairs slowly, because her head was swimming. When she reached the bottom, she crumpled, legs folded under her, and slept, her head against his bloody heart.

MONDAY

Margaret woke. Bernie didn't.

She broke her face away from his chest, where the blood had crusted. She picked up the gun. Loaded it.

It's never easy, loading a shotgun with one hand, but she used the crook of her arm, and she did it. Margaret was never surprised by the things she could do. She just did them. Like she what she was going to do now. She didn't wonder about it, she just set out to do it.

Except they denied her even that.

When she got to the field, it was all but empty. Muddy ruts crisscrossed the field. Shit and rubbish littered the mud. But there were no vans. No people.

Just a lone horse, grazing idly.

There was something flapping from the saddle. A fine saddle. Thick polished leather, ornate metalwork.

Margaret walked up to the horse. Her blood was quick with rage. But calm, too, outside. Cold, solid, calm.

"Fair's fair," said the note. The script was sprawling, shaky. An old woman's hand.

She could almost hear her, her voice echoing in the wind.

"Fair's fair," she said.

Margaret laughed as she put the gun to the horse's head and pulled the trigger.

* * *

She never did call the police.

"No point with the gypos, ma'am," they would say.

So she laughs.

She drove home, stuffed the hole in her husband's chest full of straw, and dragged him into the field, laughing the whole time.

She still laughs.

People say, "She's been so much brighter since her husband went away." People say, "Strange, how she takes such good care of that scarecrow, but never does no planting no more." People say,

"Damn crows seem to love that scarecrow."

Nobody pries. When there are miles of flat land between houses, in a land that shuns trees, people don't pry. Why would they? There's nothing in the way. They can see all they need to see from a distance.

That's the way Margaret likes it.

Things look better from a distance.

Things smell better from a distance.

Who cares what people say?

People say most anything and Margaret pays them no mind. She's got her coffee, and her farm, and she's not afraid of anything anymore, because she's got a scarecrow.

What's a scarecrow for, if not for scaring the bad things away?

THE MADNESS

Robert Essig

Chapter 1
Into the storm

Tony damned himself for getting caught in the snow, but he had no choice. The bank closed at five and the storm was blowing in much quicker than the meteorologist's forecast said it would. If there was one thing Tony should have known by now it was to never trust the weathermen. It seemed to be the only job where a person could be wrong at least ninety-nine percent of the time and yet not be fired.

The streets were a mess of sludgy ice and fresh powder creating a deadly combination even for locals who were use to dealing with such volatile driving conditions.

Heading down Main Street, he could see that the drug store was swamped with people scrambling for last minute items like batteries, water, candles and food. According to the meteorologist this was going to be one of the biggest storms Colorado had seen in recent years. And if it wasn't, one could only assume the weatherman was in bed with the owners of the drug and grocery stores with the way storm talk brought the customers in.

Tony had plenty of supplies at home, if it came to that. He was the kind of guy who lived up to the boy-scout motto: be prepared. What he *wasn't* prepared for was the early onslaught of the storm.

Traffic was unusually heavy for such shitty weather. The ferocity of the storm seemed to have caught everyone by surprise. The fast food restaurants had at least five cars in line at the drive-thru windows; the supermarket had a parking lot of cars worthy of a Saturday afternoon, all gathering a sheath of snow, thicker by the minute.

A good storm sure could bring the people out of the woodworks, especially one that was expected to turn into a full-blown blizzard. At least that's what Tony heard on the radio.

"Yeah right," said Tony as he merged into the lane that would connect him to the SR 54. "Probably be nothing but a good snow-

48

storm."

But talk of a blizzard that would supercede the holiday blizzards of 2006 was enough to cause unprepared people to stock up on goods, and stock up they did. It was rare that the snow would become so horrendous that people were trapped in their homes, but it wasn't out of the question considering the thirty to sixty inches that shut down major highways back in '06 and '03.

Tony started up the SR 54, which wound through the hills to the nearly unmapped town he lived in, if you could call it a town. With a population of 304 and the nearest neighbor five miles away, Mountain Ridge was hardly more than a village.

SR 54 was known to get bad in this kind of weather, but it wasn't anything Tony hadn't experienced before. This marked his seventh winter in Colorado, and nothing could match the blizzard of March 2003, Denver getting a whopping eighty-seven inches of snow! For a native San Diegan, that was one hell of a storm, and quite an introduction to Colorado.

About ten miles down the road Tony started having second thoughts. His tires began to slide; the snow came down in thick white sheets drowning visibility.

I've got to get home, he thought. *I cannot get stuck out here. It can't happen; It's simply not an option.*

Take it easy, man. Just take it slow, one thing at a time. That was what his brother would have said had he been in the passenger seat. Of course, he would have been so stoned by this point from the joint he would have undoubtedly lit as soon as they got in the car that he couldn't have cared less. Ignorance is bliss, right?

Forget about Randy, Tony's inner voice said. *Watch the road and lets get through this. Leave Randy back in Ohio where he belongs.*

The weather became fiercer by the minute. Tony was in the middle of a snow globe as it was shaken violently by the invisible hand of God, everything becoming white. At this point he wasn't sure his windshield wipers were doing anything at all. The white spears on either side of the road that once were trees now acted as his only guides in what was quickly becoming a vast white world.

The car caught a patch of black ice and fishtailed. Tony took his foot off the accelerator but was hesitant about hitting the break for fear that would send him into a full spinout. As the car straightened, he dropped his speed to a crawl. Visibility was about, four inches or so. It was a miracle Tony was still on the road.

With at least thirty miles or more before reaching his cozy, two-story home nestled solitarily in the Colorado hills, it would take him at least an hour and a half, and that was if the storm didn't get any worse. He realized, too, that he was driving *into* the storm.

There was no other way to get home, so he had to keep on truckin' as the saying went. How much longer he could truck before sliding into a tree or getting stuck, he wasn't sure, and becoming stuck in a mounting blizzard was a death sentence.

It's cool, man. We got this thing.

I, not we, have got this thing under control, Tony corrected Randy's voice. Ever since Ohio, Randy started speaking in his subconscious. At times, he even wondered if the poor schmuck was haunting him. He hardly had control over it. The voice would make an annoying comment whenever Tony was in a pickle, and now, in the rough of the storm, it was terribly irritating, which was exactly how Randy had been, if anything at all, when he was alive.

Give me a break, man . . .

"Shut up."

Come on, man, chill out.

"Shut up!"

Silence. That did the trick. The last thing Tony needed was to deal with his personal demons while fighting his way through an oncoming blizzard. Randy had been a pain in the ass in Ohio and Tony wasn't about to deal with his shit here in Colorado, too.

"Oh shit!" The car slid again, nearly careening into a tree. Letting off the gas, Tony allowed the car to come to a complete stop, fairly certain that no one would be on the road in front or behind him. At least that's what he hoped. He was on the road though, caught in town because he had to close the bank up for the storm, and certainly someone else could be in a similar situation. Someone driving blindly on the same road, someone who got a bite to eat at McDonalds just after buying batteries and an extra case of beer at the drug store.

That didn't matter though. Nothing would matter if he crashed his car. The chance that he would be discovered and rescued before hypothermia and frostbite killed him would be nil. In a blizzard, there wouldn't be a plow on the road until the heart of the storm passed, and that could be a day or more, assuming the plows would clear SR 54 first, which they likely wouldn't. After the nearly eight feet of snowfall in 2003 it had been days before the plows cleared SR 54. The population of Mountain Ridge is only 304 after all. The little people of small communities tend to be forgotten in the wake of a natural disaster.

It's not an option, he reminded himself. That was a mantra of his. One that he used a lot when Randy and he were in Ohio, one that now seemed to call forth Randy's voice whenever he said it; one that called out for Randy's asinine hippy mantra: *Hey, man, just go with the flow*.

The wind blew in rattling gusts, driving chunks of ice and snow into the car like pieces of shrapnel. If Tony went with the flow, he would be going right down the hill into the forest. The car was slipping very badly now. He damned himself for not carrying a set of chains in the trunk. How could he be so stupid? What happened to all that be prepared shit?

I should have closed the bank earlier, he thought. It would have helped, but under the circumstances, he had been unable to. Fifteen minutes wouldn't have hurt though, and that would have put him fifteen minutes further up the road. Either way, he would still have to deal with the wind, snow and ice. The real solution would have been to close the bank yesterday.

Another ten minutes down the road (ten minutes that felt like an hour), Tony could make out the shape of a mailbox standing in the snow like an inverted, oversized white sledgehammer. There was a serious decision to be made and time was short. Should he ask for the kindness of strangers to allow him to share their roof until the storm passed, or should he keep on truckin'?

It was no decision at all. He turned the wheel toward the mailbox in attempt to drive down what he hoped was the driveway. As he turned the wheel, his tires caught an icy patch and slid the rear end of the car into the mailbox taking it down like a bowling pin. There was a slight slope to the driveway, just enough to continue the car in its slide, a slide that was gaining momentum.

Panicking, Tony tapped his break ever so slightly but all it did was put the car into a spin causing it to slide sideways. The slant of the driveway seemed to be leveling off, but with his momentum that didn't matter.

Ahead he could see the shape of the house looming from the snowy surroundings like a monster, icicles hanging from the eaves like jagged teeth.

Oh shit, this is not an option! He was headed straight for a truck that looked like a Ford F-250, but was probably nothing more than a Ranger cloaked in a snowy disguise.

Not an option. I can't hit the truck.

Even if the people who lived there were hospitable, they would be pissed off that someone slid off the road into their truck and doubly pissed off when the idiot asked if he could stay and wait out the storm.

Just cool it, man, go with the flow, Randy piped in. *You aren't gonna hit the truck.*

"Shut up, Randy!" Tony yelled as he grabbed the steering wheel and cranked it, launching the car further into a spin. In doing so, he avoided the truck by no more than a centimeter landing his car into a large shrub.

Tony opened the door and stepped out into a white world, dazed, the wind so fierce it almost blew him down, the snow hitting his face like tiny shards of glass. Wasting no time worrying about his car or admiring Mother Nature at work, he shut the door and headed for the house taking steps like walking on the moon.

As he came closer, he could make out a shape in the window. Perhaps they had heard his crash into the bushes. He hoped so, and he hoped above all that they would welcome him to stay for a day or two. How could they not in this kind of weather? That would be inhumane.

At the door, just as Tony was about to press the doorbell, the porch light came on. It cast a strange glow through the icicles hanging from it. The door opened revealing a large man with a black beard dressed in blue jeans and a thick red flannel jacket. He looked like a lumberjack.

The man made no immediate offer of welcome.

Chapter 2
Oh, I know you

Tony stood on the front porch, a chill tightening the muscles of his exposed fingers. He had expected a hearty 'come on in out of the snow,' but the lumberjack stared at him as if he were a cop presenting a warrant for the man's arrest.

"Sir," Tony said. "I have found myself caught in the blizzard—it sure did come a lot faster that they predicted on the news—and I live about thirty miles north. I can't make it home. I was—"

"Yeah, you almost hit my truck." The man stretched his head out a little further looking in the direction of Tony's car. "Looks like you damn near took out my Juniper."

I'm glad he can't see the mailbox from here, Tony thought. "I'm terribly sorry about that, sir. I caught some black ice and slid the whole way down the driveway."

Tony began shivering. He was dressed warm, but without mittens and a beanie he couldn't keep his body heat from escaping. The lumberjack was looking at his front yard for damage as if he wanted something to bitch at Tony about.

"Do you think I can come in? It's really cold out here."

The man thought about it as if he would possibly refuse to help Tony. "Yeah, come on in," the man said in a deep baritone.

Tony wasn't as welcomed as he hoped, but in was in, and in was out from the cold and the snow. And even a mildly unfriendly house was better than freezing to death.

Tony followed the silent stranger down a hall trying to look at the pictures that adorned the walls without gazing too long. He didn't want to look like he was casing the joint. The man was hard to read and Tony was going to have to watch it until he knew the vibe of the place. By the look of the pictures, there was a Mrs. Lumberjack and a little boy. What a relief.

"Honey, is there someone out there?" asked a female voice from the living room. "Let them in. They can't stay out there in the snow."

It almost sounded as if she thought her husband had the kind of lukewarm heart that would actually let someone stay out in the snowstorm before she insisted he let them in.

"I let him in. He damn near hit my truck you know."

Clearly, the man wasn't crazy about his uninvited guest.

"Dan, what do you expect?" she said. "There's ice all over the road out there."

Dan entered the living room with Tony in tow. The room was very comfortable, clean and decorated nicely. Dan's wife sat on a couch watching the latest news about the snowstorm. The little boy he had seen in the pictures was reading a comic book on the other end of the couch.

She stood up and smiled, a polar opposite of her stuffy husband. "Oh, I know you. You're the guy from the bank, aren't you?"

Tony's face melted. He didn't like being recognized, especially by Lumberjack Dan's wife. Tony nodded. Dan looked angry, but that wasn't far from his natural facial expression.

"What's your name? Tommy, something like that?" she asked.

"Tony."

"Tony, that's right. I haven't seen you in a while. Do you still work there?"

"Yes. I'm the assistant manager now." The conversation caused him increased discomfort and nervousness, or maybe it was the way she was looking at him. Compared to Lumberjack Dan, Tony looked like GQ material. Regardless, the last thing he wanted was to be recognized. Had he known this would happen, he would have risked hypothermia.

There was an awkward silence as she stared into his eyes like a teenage girl stares at the picture of her favorite singer. She didn't just remember him because he worked at the bank, but also because she was attracted to him.

She wants to jump your bones, little bro, the maddening voice of Randy said in Tony's mind. *When he goes to sleep you can tap that, man. You know she wants it.*

"I didn't catch your name," Tony said, more to keep Randy's voice from his tormented brain than to break the silence.

"Suzie, but everybody calls me Sue."

"Well it's nice to meet you, Sue and Dan, and I hate to inconvenience you, but I'm afraid I have no other choice than to ask if I

54

may stay here until the storm passes."

"Of course you can, Tony. Isn't that right, Dan?" She looked at her husband, a look on her face that knew he wasn't crazy about the idea.

"Can't exactly send him out in the snow, now can we." That was about as close to a warm welcome as Dan seemed capable.

"Thank you very much. You don't know how much this means to me, and as a sign of my gratitude, consider me the dishwasher." Tony presented them with a smile that melted Sue's heart and did nothing more than cause Dan to feel a mild pity for him.

"Oh, you don't have to do that," said Sue. "It's our pleasure to have you here. You must be hungry. Can I fix you something to eat?"

"He'll eat what's left over from dinner," Dan bellowed.

"That's fine by me," Tony said, trying desperately not to piss Dan off.

"Why don't you go and get the day bed set up for him in the spare bedroom," Dan said to his wife. "We're gonna have ourselves a talk if you don't mind."

It was clear that Sue disliked the stern manner in which Dan spoke to her, almost as if he was her father, but nonetheless he was the man of the house, the breadwinner, and she would obey.

"Sure, hon. I'll get the room ready for him," she said, the glee completely removed from her voice. She walked down the hall into the spare bedroom leaving Dan and Tony in the living room with her comic-enthralled son.

Dan turned facing his son. "Son, this is Tony. He's gonna be staying with us for a few days. Tony, this is my son, Phillip. He mostly sits and reads comic books, but he's a good kid."

"Hi, Phillip." Tony offered his hand. Phillip shook it.

"Nice to meet you, Tony." Phillip smiled politely. Though he read many comic books, he also read print books and was quite intelligent for his ten years of age, one of the few kids to have favored other forms of entertainment to that of the television and computer.

"Lets go into the kitchen. I think I might have something to warm your belly," said Dan.

Tony followed him into the kitchen. He couldn't believe how unemotional Dan was. The man spoke in a depressing near-monotone grumble. He seemed perpetually pissed off, which made him hard to read. Tony knew what 'something to warm your belly' meant and hoped Dan wasn't one of those people who became even angrier when intoxicated.

"Have a seat," Dan pointed to a small oak dinner table with matching oak chairs. Tony obliged.

Reaching for the highest cabinet, Dan produced a bottle of Jack Daniels and two shot glasses. He placed the drinking paraphernalia on the table and took a seat directly opposite of Tony. He grabbed the half full bottle and poured out two shots.

The silence was maddening, but Tony didn't know how to break it, or perhaps he didn't want to break it. He wasn't sure. Dan stared at him as if expecting him to speak, his eyes dark and cold, the flesh beneath them sagging like a hound dog's jowls. His stare in combination with his beard made him appear frighteningly like Charles Manson.

"Shall we have a toast?" Tony offered.

3
A shot of Jack

Dan grabbed one of the shot glasses dwarfing it with his large, thick fingers and raised it. Tony did the same.

"What do you want to toast to?" Dan asked, eyes deep and piercing.

Without hesitation, Tony replied, "To the storm. It has brought us together, therefore I think it would be an appropriate cheer." It sounded cheesy, but would have to do.

Dan's Manson-eyes never changed. "To the storm," he said. They clinked shot glasses, tipped their heads back and downed the firewater.

Tony had expected Dan to slam his glass on the table like a man in a drinking contest, but he simply set the glass down and poured another. Holding the open bottle he nodded indicating for Tony to set his glass on the table so he could pour him another as well.

"So what do you do, Dan, for a living?" asked Tony.

"Auto Mechanic in town. Now we're going to cheer to my house, and the rules of the house." Dan lifted his glass.

Tony had tried to change the conversation into something more tangible, something strangers talk to one another about, but he wasn't expecting this curve ball. *Just go with the flow, man.* This time Randy's free to be, hug a tree, you and me advice was welcomed.

Tony lifted his glass. "To your house and the rules of the house." They clinked glasses and drank.

Tony hoped it would be the last shot for a while. He had given up drinking several years ago, and it was all he could do to keep his composure. The Jack Daniels was hell in his stomach, and after the second shot he knew Dan would be able to tell by Tony's constant blinking that his eyes were watering.

Dan smiled at the sight of Tony's uncomfortable appearance. It was the first sign of any emotion north of anger.

"Now you listen to me, and you listen good," Dan said.

4
Brain-tickle

Dan's mind was already swimming in a pool of intoxication when Tony arrived at his doorstep. He was drinking more heavily than usual because of the brain-tickle. His father first told him about the brain-tickle over the prison phone many years ago. And now, whenever Dan felt the tickle in his brain, he drank. Partly in attempt to drive the tickle away, but mostly to forget that day his father let the proverbial cat out of the bag. That day, Dan stared through the plexi-glass at the seemingly healthy and stable man that was his father, who basically told him his life was ruined by creed. It was the last time he saw his father alive. After being told about his future, Dan refused to visit the man again.

Dan was twenty-one the day he found out about the family madness, now forty-five and raising a family. He never felt the brain-tickle until he was about thirty-eight and up until then, he thought his father was full of shit.

"Son, let me tell you something. You know why I'm in here and yet you still come to visit me?" Jasper, his father, said all those years ago.

"Of course, pop," Dan, age twenty-one, replied.

"Well, there's somethin' you oughta know about the Ritter family—we're cursed." Dan was shocked and amused at his father's words. "I did it, son, but . . . well, it was the brain-tickle. Have you ever felt it before?"

"No. I don't know what you're talking about."

"You will, Son, you will. It tickles inside your skull like you have maggots in yer head, and it makes you think crazy thoughts."

"What are you talking about, pop? Do they have you on some kind of new medication in there?"

Jasper laughed a smoker's laugh. "No, Son, there's no medication that can help me; you either. All Ritter men have it going back before your great grandfather. I didn't listen to your grandfather when he told me. I was a lot like you. Let me tell you, son, the

59

Ritter madness got me locked up in here. I did what I did because of that madness and nothing else. I loved your mother dearly, you know that, and your brother too, but . . . ."

"What are you saying? There's a history of insanity in our family?"

Jasper nodded, his hand holding the black prison phone in a sweaty grip. Dan didn't know what to think. He wasn't even sure why he visited his father, convicted murderer of his brother and mother, and now this. It sounded like Jasper was making an excuse for his actions.

"You're makin' it up. I don't know why you killed Mom and Greg, but you're not crazy."

"Not now. It comes and goes, but it always ends in murder. I never told you, but you grandfather murdered your grandmother, and your great grandfather killed his neighbor's family. I didn't believe it until I felt the tickle for myself. Even then, I didn't believe it. Now look at me. I ask you, son, don't get married and don't have children. You're the last Ritter. You can stop the family madness."

Dan sat there looking at his father through the glass wall, phone to his ear, speechless. He didn't know what to make of it. He thought of his girlfriend (now wife), Suzie, about how he was thinking of asking her to marry him, about his future, and his father was going to give him such dire advice through the walls of a prison! Dan was supposed to take life advice from a multiple murderer? He thought not.

"I have to go, pop." He put the phone down and stood, watching his father yelling on the other side of the glass. Jasper wasn't angry—he was concerned.

Now, in the kitchen of the house he and Sue built, Dan thought of that concern and knew it to be genuine. For some years now he had known that what his father told him was true. He also knew that his son would be damned to the same awful curse, and like himself, his father before him and his grandfather before *him*, Phillip wouldn't listen to Dan's warnings.

That was one story, and the other was the arrival of a stranger in the snow. Why, on a night when Dan could feel the crawling of maggots in the space between his brain and his skull, did Tony have to walk into his life? It complicated things dearly. On a normal brain-tickle night, Dan would drink himself stupid and pass out for fear that if he didn't, he may have a taste of the ole family madness; but now, his tortured brain was tickling and dancing strange thoughts, strange ideas about this Tony fellow sitting in the chair before him.

Dan needed to talk to him, to let him understand the situation. He wouldn't mention the madness of course—his wife and son didn't even know about that—he just wanted to make sure Tony was on the same level he was. He wanted to make sure Tony knew his boundaries in the Ritter house.

5

A fair warning

"Now you listen to me, and you listen good," Dan said. His words were laced with venom. Dan leaned back to look through the living room and down the hall making sure Sue was still preparing the spare bedroom.

"I saw the way she looked at you, remembered your name, and I have to say I don't like it at all. We have a good life here. I have a good boy and a good wife, and I don't want some sharp dressed, sissy-boy fuckin' banker to come in here and ruin things."

"Dan," Tony put his hands up in surrender. "I wouldn't do anything to upset your family; I just need a place to stay for a night or two, that's all. You have to underst—"

"I don't gotta understand nothin'. *You* gotta understand that we're alone in this house for two days, maybe three," Dan lowered his voice, "and if you fuck up, I'll kill you."

Speechless, Tony held eyes with the madman.

"I saw the way she looked at you, and I'm not sure what her intentions are. You just watch yourself, you hear me? Watch yourself."

What was Tony supposed to say to that? Here he was trying to be nice by having a drink with a strange man and this was what he got, threats. Why Dan was so jealous, Tony didn't know. The lumberjack (mechanic) had issues and Tony was beginning to wish he had opted to stay in his car. Hypothermia may be a better way to go than at the hands of a drunken, jealous husband.

Hey, man, you got it made. Take care of this guy. He's no threat. Take care of him banker style, you know, like an upset customer. Once again, Randy the insufferable junkie came to the rescue.

"Look, Dan," Tony saw the bottle and decided there was no better way to gain Dan's trust than through his palate for whiskey. Tony poured two shots. "Here's to your house and its preservation." They drank without clinking glasses.

"Dan, I'm not here to invade. I just need a place to stay. When she's done fixing the room up, I can stay there if you like. Doesn't matter to me. I have absolutely no intention of getting in the way or screwing anything up. Your life's your life and it'll stay that way, I promise you."

Dan stared at Tony unblinking, his beard hiding the subtle features that could tell Tony more about his mood. A bearded man is always the hardest to read, especially one who has an affinity for anger.

Dan extended his hand. Tony shook it.

"Fair enough," Dan said. The tickle was subsiding but only a little. As soon as the booze wore off it would get worse. The only thing that seemed to drive it away was sleep, and to sleep when Dan's mind was a torrent of nasty, paranoid thoughts about his family was impossible. That's why he had to pass out. It was the only way to prevent the madness from taking over, the only way to prevent what deep down in the darkest nook of the darkest corner of his heart he knew would eventually happen.

"Then we're done here," Dan said standing from the oak table. He grabbed the bottle of Jack and took a deep pull from it. He screwed the cap on staring at Tony through red watery eyes, eyes that said, 'don't fuck with me.' He turned and walked into the living room. "There's leftovers in the fridge," he said over his shoulder.

'Okay,' Tony mouthed, wide-eyed and scared. At this point he didn't even want to see Sue, but she would be finished in the guest room only too soon and would no doubt offer to warm the leftovers for him.

Not an option, Tony thought reaching for the refrigerator handle. After the ice cold welcome, he couldn't help but feel strange looking in Dan's fridge. What was allowed to him in this refrigerator? The food in the Tupperware must have been the leftovers. It looked awful. Lifting the lid he was happy with the report from his nose.

Looks good to me, man, let's eat! Randy again. He would have eaten it without giving it a smell check, that was for sure. The dumb bastard would eat anything. "Sure Randy," Tony whispered. "Let's eat."

He placed the Tupperware bowl in the microwave and set it for two minutes wondering what he was supposed to drink. There was soda and beer in the fridge, but he was damned if he was going to ask Dan if he could have one.

"I could have warmed that up for you," Sue's voice said from behind him.

"That's all right," Tony said turning to face her. He hoped she couldn't see the weariness in his eyes.

"Well, can I get you something to drink? A soda, a beer?"

He didn't know how to answer. He wanted a soda, but didn't want Dan freaking out in the next room listening to their small talk. "A soda sounds good."

"Okay."

An all too familiar beep rang out from the microwave indicating that it was finished heating the food. Tony opened the small door and removed the Tupperware bowl setting it on the counter. He reached for a drawer, not wanting to ask Sue where the silverware was, just as she turned to grab a glass from the cabinet, bumping heads like the two stooges.

"Oh, I'm sorry," she said giggling.

"No, I'm sorry, I didn't see you there."

She giggled and he didn't like it. He felt as if Dan would come rushing into the kitchen and clobber him over the head with a whiskey bottle.

"I'm so clumsy," Sue said. "I'm really sorry. How's your head feel?"

"It's fine. Do you think I can eat this in my room?"

"You can eat on a TV tray in the living room if you like. We always do. There's no TV in the spare bedroom."

She was hard to deny being such a hospitable soul. If only her lumberjack-looking husband was the same way this wouldn't be such a bad gig.

"C'mon, Tony, we wouldn't want you to have to sit in that room without anything to do. Why don't you come in here with us and watch some TV." She walked into the living room. "Here," her voice called over the din of the television. "I'll get a TV tray ready for you."

"Damn-it, Sue, he can get it himself. Why are you caterin' to 'im anyway? Ya damn fool idiot."

Now Tony *really* didn't want to join the Ritter family. Dan was pissed, and he didn't want to see what was to become of the man after the whiskey kicked in.

64

Chapter 6
Is he always like this?

Tony stalled as long as he could without seeming too timid before entering the living room. The room was foreign to him since he had only seen it on his arrival. There was a couch, a love seat and a recliner. He was happy to see that Sue had set up the TV tray on the vacant love seat. He didn't want to sit next to their son, nor did he want to sit next to Sue, and he sure as hell didn't want to sit next to Dan and his good friend Jack Daniels.

Tony set the bowl on the tray noticing that he had forgotten something.

"Shoot, I forgot to get a fork."

"I'll get you one," Sue said, already halfway to the kitchen before Tony could object.

He took a deep breath and let it out slowly chancing a glance in Dan's direction. Dan stared at him tight-lipped like Popeye's nemesis, Bluto, all evil and nasty. The bottle of whiskey had considerably less liquor in it than it had when Bluto left the kitchen.

He's a monster, a crazy, whiskey-drinking monster.

Sue returned with the fork. "Here you go, and I brought you some salt."

"Thanks."

On the TV was one of CNN's talking heads commenting on the war in the Middle East and how the president was handling it. Was Dan even watching this? As Tony ate the food and drank his soda, he could feel Dan's eyes like laser beams. Obviously he wasn't watching the TV. He was watching Tony eat.

It's getting tense, man. You gotta break the monotony. Say somethin', man, anything. If there was one thing back in Ohio that would frighten Tony, it was when Randy felt tense. Randy was calm and cool by nature. He was a dyed in the wool stoner from head to toe. The man spent his life in a constant state of sedation. When Randy felt tense, the shit really must be about to hit the fan.

Randy's dead, Tony reminded himself, but that didn't matter.

They had spent many years living together in a broken down, nine hundred square foot shack of a house in Ohio and if the voice of Randy in his head was feeling tense, the situation needed to be dealt with.

"This is really good, Sue, and I mean that. It's delicious."

She smiled. "You like it, really?" She wasn't used to getting compliments. Dan and Sue's relationship was many years past the time of compliments. To Dan it was the same food he had been eating for the past twenty years. It was good today and it was good back then, and if it got bad, *then* he'd say something. Phillip emulated his father as far as bad manners went. Like father like son and all.

"Tomorrow I'm making baked chicken with white rice and a mushroom sauce. It isn't anything special, but I hope you like it."

"Special," Dan muttered throwing back a swig of whiskey. "Same damn thing we have every week. No, nothin' special."

Tony noticed that Sue seemed to pay no mind to her husband's outbursts. She just ignored him. Tony wondered if Dan was always like this. How could such a lovely woman live in such a mentally abusive household? Why should Tony wonder? There were households all over America suffering far worse afflictions. Some women got into ugly situations under the guise of something good and became trapped by fear. Tony wouldn't be the slightest bit surprised to find out that Dan beats her. Probably has bruises on her back and thighs where no one will ever see them.

The room was no less tense, maybe more so since Tony's compliment. He couldn't think of an icebreaker that would bring everyone together into a tangible conversation. In Dan's twisted condition Tony wasn't sure there was any way to reduce the thick fog of distress that filled the living room and stifled any chance at relaxation.

Tony finished eating, Sue changed the channels of the TV, and Dan stared at the man who walked into his home on the wrong day, the day of the brain-tickle. Dan stared at the stranger in his house as if Tony's presence was a scar.

"What are you staring at, Dan?" Sue asked. "You're starting to freak me out, and probably Tony too. You've been staring at him the whole time he ate his dinner. How's the man supposed to eat his dinner with you looking psychotic and staring."

Dan was sensitive to certain adjectives like: crazy, psycho, nuts, loony, etcetera. When he would act like this, many times after drinking too much, those were the words that seemed best to define his actions. Those were also the words that got he and Sue into violent yelling matches. Nothing physical, but violent nonetheless.

"What have I told you 'bout talking like that 'bout me?" Dan said.

"Dan, look, I'm sorry. I didn't mean to say that, but here we've got a guest and you're sitting there staring at him and chugging that bottle. Do you think you can calm down, please?"

Dan looked from Sue to Tony. He took another pull, much too quickly, causing him to spit into the neck of the bottle, liquor dripping down his beard onto his flannel shirt. For a moment he had a look of bewilderment to him.

Sue put her head into her hands not wanting to look at her disgrace of a husband. Tony noticed Phillip, who had been so completely absorbed by his comic books, now staring at his father, eyes welled with tears on the verge of spilling down his face like miniature faucets. How terrible it was for the poor child to have to be subjected to such a rotten father.

"Phillip, why don't you go to your room to read your comic books?" Sue said softly, her voice quivering.

Phillip grabbed his comics and disappeared down the hall. He had seen the scenario play out before. Tony heard Phillip sniffle and knew he wouldn't be doing any reading in his room. More likely he would try to listen to his parents fighting, something he had probably done time and again in the past.

"I think maybe it would be a good idea if I turn in for the night," said Tony. "I just want to put the day behind me if you know what I mean." Tony stood, stretching and yawning though he really wasn't tired at all.

Sue nodded as a tear ran down her face. "There'll be breakfast in the morning."

"Bre'fust, huh!" Dan looked Tony in the eyes, freezing him with a Medusa stare. "'Member . . . I warned you, you jest 'member."

"Here, I'll show you to your room." Sue walked down the hall, Tony behind her.

The room was next to the bathroom and across the hall from Phillip's room. She had set up a fold out bed with fresh linens and two pillows. The room was cozy, a chair in the corner, and bookshelves along the wall.

"It looks nice," Tony whispered.

He saw in her eyes that she knew perfectly well why he whispered.

"I'm so sorry about Dan, I . . . " she trailed off.

"Is he always like this?"

"No," she answered quickly, maybe too quickly. "Only sometimes, when he drinks too much. He's never harmed us, but he gets mad. He gets jealous over nothing and accuses me of things I didn't do. I don't know why, but I can guarantee you he'll be better tomorrow. He always is. On nights like this he's like Dr. Jekyll and Mr. Hyde."

"That's strange. He only gets like this every once and a while?" Tony asked. She nodded. "I guess I picked the wrong snow storm to get stranded in." She smiled at his remark and that was what he was looking for. "Well, you better go, I don't want him getting any ideas."

"Goodnight, Tony. Like I said, I'll make breakfast in the morning, probably about nineish."

"Goodnight."

She exited the room, closing the door behind her, leaving Tony to reflect on his past few hours in the Ritter home and the words Dan spoke to him, slurred and drunk, just before he followed Sue down the hall. A nice woman and a nice boy living with a monster of multiple personalities: Drunk by night; good guy by day.

He's crazy, little bro, there's nothin' to it. He's zonkers. The bad thing about solitude was the ever-persistent Randy who, like a loud-mouthed ghost, rattled off in his consciousness as if he were right there in the room, and it was becoming worse. *I'm right here, bro, always, and that cat's not right.*

Right or wrong, there was little Tony could do. By this time his car would be buried beneath two feet of snow and even if it wasn't, there would be no way to drive through SR 54 until after the storm. Even then he would have to wait for the plows. How long would that be? Two, three days at the most. There was one hell of a storm out there, maybe worse than '03, and it could be four or five days until the roads were clear.

Tony sat in the room glancing at the titles on the bookshelves, wishing for coffee. The shots of Jack Daniels were drowsing his worried mind. With a maniac in the house drunk off his gourd, sleep was the last thing Tony wanted.

Randy's chuckle rose in the back of Tony's mind, dancing

through his thoughts like the Cheshire cat's eyes through Wonderland. Tony knew that laugh, that stoner chuckle, very well. If something could be medicated through means of illegal (sometimes legal) drugs, Randy was an underground pharmacist.

Bennies, Nodoz, yellow jackets, meth . . . The voice rattled off at least a dozen means of staying awake, none of which helped Tony. The room was all books and a bed and he didn't dare use the restroom, not yet at least. In the medicine cabinet he may find something that would suffice, but until then, he was going to have to find a good book, which would be tricky. Even a good book was apt to make him drowsy.

If only there was a goddamn T.V. in here.

Tony found a book with a strange cover displaying two monkeys holding their hands out through what appeared to be prison bars. The book was *Welcome to the Monkey House* by Kurt Vonnegut, Jr. It wasn't until he was half way through the second chapter before he realized it wasn't a novel, but a collection of short fiction, and pretty good too. Good enough to keep his ears awake and tuned to the silence of the house. If the silence were to be disturbed, he wanted to know why.

After an hour and a half, Tony began to relax. By now Dan was no doubt passed out for the night, hopefully in bed and not on the couch. Sometimes when drunks woke from a long pass out on the couch they were liable to stir the shit up again.

He lay there on the bed after reading the first five stories from the Vonnegut volume, especially liking the title story, when he began to consider the consequences of his situation. He hoped Sue was right that her husband would be cured of his rotten temper and drinking habit after a good night sleep, but he had his doubts.

It just wasn't right. People don't start drinking all of the sudden like a weredrunk at the sight of a full moon. It just isn't in the human condition. Perhaps she was lying to him for his safety? But she did seem to believe what she was saying. Maybe she was in denial. Maybe Dan was like that every night of their lives and every night after he passed out she told herself that he would be normal in the morning. Tony wouldn't put it past her.

Denial is a strong coping mechanism.

Tony turned the light off half expecting to see a faint glow under his door from the light in the living room, but everything was pitch black.

He turned his light back on, then opened the door. The house was silent and dark. He used the bathroom after which he returned to his room and read another story from his selected volume.

With the drunk asleep, all was well. Even Randy's voice wasn't getting a word in.

7
The first morning

Sue woke at seven thirty like always, Dan next to her snoring where he would lay sleeping for at least another three hours, maybe four. On a drunk like the one he was on last night, he was going to be out for a long time.

She hoped Tony would be awake. She wanted to talk to him about last night before Dan woke. She could clue him in on their situation a lot better knowing that she had time to talk without being rudely interrupted by a raving drunk.

The air outside the warmth of the flannel sheets and covers was a death chill. Opposite of the Folgers coffee ads it was the worst part of waking up. Nonetheless, she had to get out of bed, make coffee (Yuban, not Folgers) and hopefully talk to Tony.

One leg crept from the desert to the arctic, then another, shivering immediately. The house was probably forty degrees or less. At least it felt that way.

The robe was secured nice and tight, the slipper socks pulled high and tucked into a thick pair of slippers; now to the bathroom. She dammed the rich for their warming towel racks and toilet seats. She had to pee like a Mare after the races. When she sat on the horseshoe shaped piece of ice that was the toilet seat she clenched up and had to relax before she could actually relieve herself.

After the bathroom, she wandered down the hall yawning and stretching herself awake. Tony's door was closed.

"Late sleeper," she mumbled.

In the living room the TV wasn't on, which was odd. Phillip was always up before dawn in his pajamas watching cartoons. It was a tried and true tradition for him.

Looking into the empty living room, she tilted her head considering how out of place she felt. She wanted to talk to a stranger they had let stay with them through the blizzard maybe more than she wanted a cup of coffee, and her son was sleeping in.

Of course he's sleeping in. Normally he would be going to

school today. He probably woke and listened to the blowing wind outside deciding to act like he hadn't woke at all in hopes that he would be forgotten about and wouldn't have to go to school, not remembering in his sleepy child brain that school was closed until the passing of the blizzard.

Sue smiled at the thought and proceeded into the kitchen to brew a pot of coffee.

On the kitchen table was something that dulled her smile: the bottle of Jack Daniels. The cap was removed, the bottle empty save for a shot and a half. Bad memories and wicked flashbacks sobered her foggy mind. Not memories from last night, last night was tame, but memories from the past four years or so. Vivid memories. Terrible memories.

She poured what little of the remaining elixir was left down the sink, then threw the bottle in the trash. Oh how she wished Tony would come waltzing into the kitchen. She would be able to make everything all right, set the stage for the day to come; let him know that things weren't as bad as they appeared.

Not with her luck. Tony was probably going to sleep as long as her husband could. *Men*, she thought.

From the kitchen sue heard the gentle bubbling of the coffee maker, not even remembering that she prepared it to brew. That's how automatic making coffee in the morning was for her, just as automatic as sitting on the frozen toilet, or Phillip watching his cartoons . . .

The coffee maker sputtered its dark brew as Sue saw the brightness of a light bulb flash in her mind. She figured out how to possibly rouse Tony from his sleep. All she would have to do was wake Phillip and remind him that he didn't have to go to school. As soon as the words left her mouth, he would jump out of bed and plant himself in front of the TV. She would let him turn the volume up a little louder than she normally would, and the sound just might wake Tony up.

"Good idea, Sue," she said to herself, walking out of the kitchen just as the coffee maker dropped the last dark drip of caffeine into the pot.

Phillip's door was ajar. She pushed it open gently not wanting him to hear her enter. She wanted to see his face when she woke him; his mind thinking it was another school day, then finding out that it wasn't. It would tickle her heart to see him so happy.

Phillip was curled in his bed merely a shape beneath the covers, probably hiding himself from the threat of another day at school. His comic books were strewn on the floor in the same pattern they were when she kissed him goodnight.

His leg twitched under the covers. What fantastic delights were surging through his mind as he lay there dreaming? Maybe he was running, but where? She could only imagine, and more than likely, her imagination couldn't fathom the wild fiction of her son's subconscious.

She reached out softly placing her hand on the shape of sheet that must have been his shoulder. He jerked like a fish out of water. At first she thought she had woke him from a deep slumber, but when he didn't stop flailing about she grabbed the covers and revealed her son bound and gagged, his eyes a wide terror stare.

Just as she opened her mouth to scream she saw her son's eyes shift to look behind her, and understood his terror as a hand came from behind and clamped onto her mouth, the other arm reaching around to restrain her arms. The arms pulled her back against the warmth of her assailant.

Phillip wiggled but couldn't move. He was secured very tightly to his bed. Sue watched and squirmed as tears wet her son's face. She bit down as hard as she could on the hand that stifled her alarming scream.

The hand clenched over her teeth very tightly, and she let out a muffled screech as pain shot through her jaw.

"Then stop biting or I'll rip your teeth out," the voice said low and cold like Clint Eastwood in *The Good The Bad And The Ugly*. "If you cooperate with me then I can make this very easy. You and Phil can live. You just have to calm down and let me tie your arms behind your back."

She squirmed and tried to scream even more at his offer for cooperation. She was a tough cookie, Sue was, and she wasn't about to let anything else happen to her son.

"Okay, should have expected a mother would want to protect her child. We'll have to do this the hard way."

Her assailant pivoted her body so that he was facing her profile. Her eyes darted in his direction just in time to recognize his face as he head butted her. She fell limp in his arms like a human rag doll. Wasting no time, he used ropes and rags to gag her and bind her appendages.

He had to work quickly; she would only be out for ten minutes at most, probably less.

Chapter 8
Is everyone awake?

Standing over the bed, he wielded a rubber mallet in one hand and a large kitchen knife in the other, at his feet more rope. With the rest of the family subdued Dan should be no problem at all, but time was short, and he would become a problem if awakened by the ruckus Sue would surely make when she woke up.

The freshly woken are always groggy when pulled from slumber delicately by a soft voice or maybe a gentle nudge, especially if the sleeper was recovering from a bad drunk the night before. The attacker used this knowledge to his advantage and played wife.

"Dan," he mimicked a woman's voice, the knife at Dan's throat. "Honey, wake up, breakfast is ready."

Dan's eyes stirred in gluey sleep. He mumbled a few incoherent words, licked his lips and let out a sigh.

"Don't you want some coffee and eggs," the impersonated voice faded into baritone. "Or would you rather have a whiskey?"

Dan's eyes popped open, his foggy half-drunk mind catching up with his survival instincts.

"Don't fuckin' move, punk." After noticing the Clint Eastwood sound in his voice with Sue, he decided to take on a half-cocked Dirty Harry tone with Dan.

"What the—" was all Dan could say.

"Were gonna do this nice and easy and I wont have to slit your throat."

The fear fled Dan's retinas replaced with primal anger. "You sonofabitch! I'll fu—"

The rubber mallet hit Dan in his temple. He was out cold before he could finish his tirade.

With the rope, the assailant bound Dan more securely than the others. He wrapped rope around Dan's ankles three fold, likewise around his wrists, and then strapped him to the bed.

"Is everyone awake?" Tony yelled at the silent house stand-

75

ing at the base of Dan's bed.

Randy laughed heartily in Tony's madcap mind. Randy would have loved tying up a whole family. Tony listened to the laughter like a hyena trapped in his cranium, and he didn't like it. It made him feel especially crazy after what he had just done. It wasn't as if Tony wanted to tie up the Ritter family.

He had to.

Chapter 9
First thing's first

The storm blew another couple of feet of snow since the night before and wasn't letting up any time soon. The wind blew hard and cold against the house rattling the windows in the morning silence.

Tony stood in front of a large picture window in the living room that faced the front yard. His car was nothing more than a white lump disguised in the snowy landscape next to the two lumps that were Dan and Sue's cars. He wanted so badly to be away from his current situation, to be at home, but . . .

But now he was in deep. Hadn't he once before been in a similar situation, a dire lapse of reason that led him in a violent direction, Randy and he? Yes, and only a few years ago it was, in Ohio. What Tony liked to refer to as The Massacre.

It was a massacre, all right, but you've got this thing covered. You're in control here. Randy always had a way to make a horrible situation seem less precarious, apparently even after his death. *How 'bout some coffee, bro?*

"Shut up," Tony whispered. Randy's recurring speech wasn't assuring Tony of his sanity, that was for sure.

He found the coffee Sue prepared and it wasn't until he was half way through his first cup that he heard the apt silence disrupted. It was Sue; it was that motherly feeling of wanting to protect her child.

"Sue, you really ought to calm down. You're not going anywhere," Tony yelled down the empty hall.

She stopped.

He decided on a breakfast of pancakes with maple syrup, butter and a large glass of milk. How he had the stomach for eating, even he didn't know, but there was a lot to do in the next few hours and he certainly didn't want to be working on an empty stomach.

* * *

First thing's first, thought Tony walking down the hallway, the taste of maple syrup on his lips. He had been staring out at the dim sky and bright white ground when he realized there was only one person in the house that was a real threat, and if things were going to fall into place the way Tony wanted them to, he was going to have to take care of business . . . after a few questions, of course.

He walked past Phillip's room, hesitated, then turned and opened the door to give the boy and his mother a word of advice. They were where he left them. Sue had apparently been banging her head on the wall earlier to get his attention for there was a crack in the plaster behind her head.

"No noise, please, no matter what you hear. No matter what! I need you to be quiet," he was looking from one to the other and now focused on Sue. "Or it's your son's ass."

He left the room heading for the master bedroom.

Chapter 10
For your family's sake

The master bedroom smelt faintly like whiskey. Tony grimaced at the way Dan's foul breath permeated the stale air in the room. The bastard probably had to take a piss by now with all he drank the night before, but Tony was in no position to let him use the bathroom. It would be far too risky. Dan would just have to suffer a bladder ache or piss himself.

Dan was awake as Tony thought he would be. The man stared up from the bed breathing through his half congested nostrils, chest rising and falling heavily.

"Look at you. You smell like a distillery," Tony said simply, noting the wild eyes that said more than words, eyes that yelled out for Tony's head on a rusty pole. "I need you to cooperate with me, for your family's sake."

Dan squirmed, yelling into the duct tape, snot furiously spitting from his nose. He cursed Tony to no avail, cursed himself as well for his twisted genes that seeded his lust for the bottle on nights like last night.

Tony pulled a butcher knife from his belt, the one that was to Dan's throat an hour ago.

"You need to calm down, Dan, for your family's sake. I just need to ask you a few questions, that's all. Just a few questions. I need you to be cooperative, and believe you me, so does your wife and son."

Dan's squirming ceased, his eyes remained afire.

Tony paced the length of the bed slapping the blade of the knife in his hand, tilting his head as if thinking of what he wanted to ask. But there was only one question on his mind.

"First," Tony stopped pacing and looked Dan square in the eyes, "I need to know where all of your weapons are. You look like a hunter, an outdoorsman, which leads me to believe that you have some guns, probably a rifle, a shotgun, or a handgun. More if you're a collector."

Their eyes were two locked pairs trying to read each other's thoughts through the retinas, like a mental cold war. Tony had the power to turn it into a hot war.

Tony looked at the knife. "I don't know how sharp you keep the kitchen knives in this house, but I guess we'll see. I'm going to cut a slit in that duct tape where your mouth is so you can speak. Yelling will do you no good."

Tony placed his free hand on Dan's head delicately but ready to use force if Dan struggled. He brought the blade of the knife to the duct tape approximately where Dan's lips would part.

"Do you keep your knives sharp?"

Tony slid the knife back and forth conducting a silent symphony. To his surprise, it was beginning to cut through the first layer of the duct tape and then through the cross grid mesh of the middle layer, the layer that makes the tape so strong.

"Your knife is good and sharp, Dan. Hopefully my cutting is to par. Just keep still."

Tony glided the knife back and forth applying little pressure letting the blade do the work, now cutting through the final layer before the flesh of Dan's lips. He held the blade as delicately as a surgeon, trying as hard as he could not to slice into tender flesh.

C'mon, man, show him who's boss. Give him a little taste of what could happen to his kid. You can't be too nice to him. You want him to bleed.

Abruptly, Tony stopped cutting. Dan's eyes widened reflecting the sudden change in Tony's demeanor.

It was Randy again. *How does that bastard get in my head?* Tony had never before heard someone's voice so full and undeniable inside the walls of his skull before. Sure, he had heard his mother nag him when he was a kid, he would even hear his father speak up, but never was the mental talk so random and independent of his own thoughts. Normally his mother's voice would ring in his head reminding him of something she had already told him, but Randy... his mental voice seemed to say whatever it wanted to. It seemed to act as if Randy were alive and sitting in the room with Tony, reflecting on the situation at hand.

Tony gripped the knife tight, knuckles whitening. Dan must have seen something in Tony's eyes because he let out a muffled scream as Tony clenched his teeth and swiped the knife like a credit card, slicing through the last layer of the tape and severing Dan's upper lip from his face.

Though he was told not to scream, even Tony couldn't scold Dan for the yell that echoed from his throat.

There was blood.

Tony wasn't ready for blood. He hadn't anticipated cutting the man's lip off. Springing back, he watched Dan yell through the slit in the duct tape, little drops or blood-spittle spraying out of his mouth like a defunct fountain. Dan squirmed like a live mummy wrapped in gray duct tape, his vocalizations prehistoric.

Tony watched . . . stared . . .

Remembered . . .

Chapter 11
Shut him up!

"Hey, Tony, why doncha calm him down, he's gettin on my nerves," Randy said from the master bedroom glazing over a meth pipe, his eyes ready to pop out of his skull and dangle over his face. "Tony! Shut him up!"

Tony hovered over the man like looming death wielding a pistol and a hunting knife. The man cowered in the corner of his kitchen dressed in slacks and a white shirt and tie: his work clothes. He had already soiled the slacks frightened to find that his home, his domain, had been intruded upon.

"Shut him up!" Randy yelled. Methamphetamine was the one drug that could turn his normally mellow mood into angry psychosis.

Tony looked at the man noting his body quivering in fear. He had gotten off on that position of making someone cower in fear, watching them shake from his wrath. He had felt superior before in a similar situation, but now he wasn't so triumphant.

He felt bad for the man below him.

"SHUT HIM UUUUUP!!!"

The man wasn't even yelping anymore. In fact, he had quieted down completely. Clearly, Randy was off on another one of his drug trips: complete psychological despair. That was the reason Tony came to grip with what was really going on. Randy had a way of making every despicable thing seem right and Tony would always go along with it whether he felt right about it or not. It wasn't as if Tony was a saint, quite the contrary, but Randy, he was fashioned from a completely different bolt of cloth, one that had surely been wrapped around the Devil's loins.

"Please," the man said. "I see you understand he's crazy. You don't have to do this, really."

Tony was confused. An intelligent man he was, but there was always a higher pedestal that he held his brother on, even though Randy was a fuck up. It must have had something to do with Randy being older. Tony idolized him when they were children and even when Randy went over the deep end, Tony always looked up to him.

Looking into the man's eyes, Tony peered into his soul searching for his own and he couldn't find it anywhere. Had he lost it? He wasn't sure he ever had one in the first place. Randy sure as hell hadn't, sitting in the master bedroom staring down on a dead woman in a pool of coagulating blood. He was as soulless as a human could be, some may go as far as calling him a demon.

"Please, don't hurt my wife. Take me instead," the man pleaded again.

It was a little too late for that. The man's wife was staring at Randy with dead eyes in the bedroom, but beyond that image, Tony saw something else in the man, a man he had never seen before, something that made him understand life in a way he had never known. This man would have given his life for his family. His wife had been gutted with a shotgun before he came home from work, but had he been there he would have sacrificed himself for her.

Tony could see that in the man's eyes, and something inside him changed. His loyalty toward his scum-fuck brother changed.

Chapter 12
New plan

That was then. Tony had had a long time to think about that night, and think about it he did all the way from Ohio to Colorado. The fast times his brother and he had in Ohio were all a faded Polaroid that had fallen between the dresser drawers of his mind, up until now.

He had straightened his life out in Colorado, years away from the life of crime he lived with Randy. Got himself a job at the local bank, worked his way up to assistant manager, and now this! How could it come to this?

You can't think about that right now, bro. You gotta get this guy in line. You gotta—

Tony was going to have to learn to use his mental block if he was going to get the situation under control, hell, if he wanted to get out of this snowstorm and free from the awful mess he created.

Dan was a fish out of water squirming in a duct tape cocoon, blood splattered across his face.

"Stop it," Tony said simply. Dan didn't hear him. He was far too focused on the quarter inch slice of flesh that dangled from his mouth. "Stop it!" Still nothing save for agonizing screams.

Tony fled to the master bathroom, opened the medicine cabinet and returned with a bottle of rubbing alcohol. He unscrewed the cap and held it over Dan's face threateningly.

"If I were you I'd shut the fuck up before I pour this over your mouth, now . . .

(shut your lip)

. . . Shut up."

Dan's eyes stared at the bottle alive with the knowledge that it would feel like acid if Tony were to pour it over his face. Tony, being only mildly sadistic, wasn't interested in the alcohol as anything more than a tool in gaining Dan's attention.

"As I was saying before: I want to know where you keep your guns. A safe? Maybe under the mattress? Where?"

"Fuck you." Dan's speech was slurred do to his new impediment.

"No, sir, it is not I who is fucked, it is you. Well," Tony glanced toward the door to the hallway. "You and your family, and if you want them to remain safe then I suggest you tell me what I want to know."

"Fuck you. I'm not saying anything."

"Saying nothing will only hurt your family, Dan, now tell me: where are your guns?"

Dan was silently contemplating his situation, the dangling piece of his lip sucking in and blowing out of his mouth with every breath.

Tony had remained reasonably calm up until now (after his lip cutting outburst), but Dan wasn't cooperating as well as he thought a man would whose family was in danger. Apparently, Dan's family didn't mean as much to him as Tony hoped.

"New plan," Tony said pacing back and forth. He stopped to look Dan in the eyes. "I'm going to search your house, and when I find your guns I am going to bring your family in here and shoot them in front of you, and I don't mean in the head. I'm going to start with their feet and arms so you can watch them suffer. Is that what you want?"

Dan's eyes were saucers in his bloodied head. As heartless an asshole as he may have been, the last thing he wanted to see was his family murdered in living Technicolor. He sat there, what was left of his upper lip throbbing with pain, wide-eyed and far too prideful to submit to Tony's demands.

"Have it your way," Tony said as he turned toward the mirrored closet doors of the master bedroom. He opened the closet and began rifling through the contents discarding boxes and clothes to the middle of the floor, searching.

"I saw the way you were so jealous last night, Dan. The mere thought of your wife even talking to me made you sick to your stomach. I didn't think you were the kind of sadist that would choose his pride over seeing his family murdered."

Tony looked through a box and tossed it aside reaching for another from the top shelf of the closet. He was mildly surprised at Dan's silence.

"You can still tell me where to find the goods, Dan. I won't penalize you either, that is, unless you are actually looking forward to watching me kill your family."

The closet was clear. If there was a gun in there it was hidden well. Tony decided to check under the bed.

Nothing.

"Last chance, Dan. I'm gonna find your guns whether you tell me where they are or not. If you tell me where they are everything will stay as it is. If I have to find them . . . well, that's gonna complicate things."

Very carefully, Dan said: "Fuck . . . you."

"Very well."

Tony opened the door and went to the kitchen for a cup of coffee then searched the attic, which was piled with boxes labeled: X-MAS and HALLOWEEN. He searched the boxes anyway and found their labels to be true.

In the attic the storm was loud, the wind whipping at the house in heavy bursts. A solitary window looked down on the front yard. Tony tried to look through it, but couldn't see past the ice that had formed over it. As the wind shifted, he could hear the snow beating upon the glass. The storm was as strong as ever, perhaps at its zenith.

Descending the ladder, the sound of the storm became muffled by the insulated walls and double paned windows, though there were a few older windows in the house that rattled incessantly. The house was supposed to be silent except for the wind and snow, but there was a whisper. A female whisper.

Tony had probably spent more time in the attic than he anticipated, but surely it wasn't enough time for Sue to escape her bondage. If so, she was one stupid bitch to think she was going to outsmart Tony.

Standing just outside Phillip's room, Tony listened to a silence indicating that Sue must have heard his descent from the attic. He decided to stand there as quietly as possible and wait for her to speak up again.

Dude, you should go in there and get her to tell you where the guns are. If you cut her kid, she'll do anything you want.

Tony hated to admit it, but Randy was right.

He waited for her to speak again but heard nothing more than the storm he so desperately wanted to end. Though he had the whole family held captive, in some way he felt like he was losing control. If only he had a gun he would feel better about waiting out

86

the storm, better about digging his car out of the snow and high-tailing it through the Colorado mountains to his house, better about fleeing America for Canada, or perhaps Mexico.

He opened the door abruptly hoping he would catch Sue in the act of escape. No such luck. She sat on the floor where he left her, hands bound behind her back, the gag in her mouth. Phillip was restrained on the bed.

"Something here is wrong. 'Cause I can swear I heard you talking, but how can that be if you're wearing your gag?"

Tony reached for her assuming she was merely holding her hands behind her back—untied—and as he did so she reached out with her fingers poised claw-like, ready to rip his eyes out. Prepared for her display of violence, Tony cracked his hand across her face; a flesh and bone whip snapping her jaw like a firecracker.

She retreated to the corner shocked, her face numb, a solitary drop of blood running from her nose. The fact that she thought she could overpower a maniac like Tony was insane. The sight of her son squirming and crying, his sobs and screams muffled in the gag, caused her to break into a fresh bout of tears.

"You are a clever one, aren't you? I don't know how you did it, but I can certainly make sure you don't get out again."

He stood over her cowering body consumed with a power he once knew, the power one feels when another is at their beck and call, when someone is scared shitless of the consequences of a hair-trigger response to the mere act of sniveling, crying, and most of all . . . trying to escape.

Hey, Tony!

Shut up!

You know—

"Shut up," Tony muttered.

What you—

"Shut up!"

Should do.

"SHUT UP!"

Tony's hand swung backward balled in a fist connecting with Phillip's face. The boy made a muffled noise, his nose now matching his mothers, swelling immediately.

"No!" Sue screamed.

"Shut up!"

I knew you knew what to do.

"Randy, shut the fuck up!"

The house was once again quiet. Probably Dan heard her scream, but what the hell, he was tied up in the master bedroom. He couldn't do anything if he tried.

As with the house, Tony's mind was silent again, Randy haven gotten his way. Somehow, someway, the poor dead bastard was snickering.

"That's for trying to escape. If I were you, I'd cooperate."

Sue bowed her head and nodded, tears flooding her face saturating the oversized nightshirt she was wearing, probably one of Dan's shirts as big as it was.

"Here," he grabbed her arm. "Come with me."

Tony walked her into the living room where he had previously piled several items he thought would come in handy during his stay at the Ritter house. Bungee cords, rope and a box of tools were amongst the items littering the living room floor, as well as a pair of handcuffs compliments of the Halloween box in the attic. Holding her arms behind her back, he cuffed her hands as tight as her wrists would allow. It wasn't likely the cuffs were authentic, but they were metal and seemed real enough.

"You could have had it comfortable, but you had to go and be a hero, didn't you."

"I wont . . . I wont try to get out again, I swear."
"Don't they always," he said dryly.

He grabbed a bungee cord from the pile and hooked one of the plastic covered metal hooks through the loop of the right handcuff.

"What're you doing?" There was an irrational sense of fear in her voice as he pulled the bungee cord up wrapping it around the front of her neck pulling her arms behind her back in an unnatural way.

"Like I said, you could have had it comfortable." Tony pulled the free end of the bungee down her back hooking it to the other cuff, rubbing it across the front of her neck as he did so. She shrieked at the burning pain. "Now you're going to have to be in pain."

As he let go of her bound hand, she fell on her side screaming. Her body contorted in a manner that gave her the appearance of perpetual agony, which wasn't far from the truth. Her head was pulled back by the bungee cord that was stretched tight around her neck connecting the left and right handcuffs, the tautness pulling her arms behind her back in a way God never intended.

Tony grabbed her arm and hauled her up to her feet. She was a mess of tears and blood and pieces of hair that had caught in the bungee cord.

"Come on. You're gonna show me where Dan keeps his guns."

He walked her back into her son's room.

Chapter 13
The guns

Once in Phillip's bedroom, Sue was on the floor where she had been seated before she came up with the crazy idea of wiggling free from her restraints and saving the day.

Tony was silent. He knew what he had to ask her, and it could get ugly if she didn't comply. He propped her in the corner like a useless passed out drunk. She remained in pain, the bungee-chord nearly cutting off her breathing. It appeared that she was refraining from movement as much as possible. By now the sweat and tears were no doubt stinging the lacerations the bungee chord caused on her neck like salt water. Moving was torture.

Tony hadn't wanted it this way, but what else was he supposed to do? If she hadn't fucked up in the first place she wouldn't be in such a tight restraint. Besides, Randy came up with the idea, and in the past it was Randy's blatant disrespect and uncouth that could take a situation and make it bleed. He was the one who could make a liberal vote for a republican or make a nun worship Satan. His ways of vice were unbelievable, wonderful and horrid all at once.

Tony never would have wrapped a bungee-cord around Suzie's neck like this—he wouldn't have dreamed something so vile. That's why he was in silence observing the situation and wondering just how it came to this. If Randy wasn't long ago dead by the bullets of Cleveland's best, Tony would have thought he was somewhere in the house with a lighter heating the underside of a glass pipe.

However, the flame was elsewhere heating the mind of Tony himself, heating it to a level of carelessness and maniacal brutality.

This wasn't Tony. Not by a long shot.

Shut up and get the guns, man, Randy said.

"That's right. I'm in it and I have to keep with it."

Tony, up to now, had been staring at the carpet unaware of his surroundings. He could have been ambushed the way he was spaced out. He now focused his attention on Sue.

"Where does Dan keep his guns? I need them."

"Dan," she was gagging on every word. "Doesn't . . . have any . . . guns."

"Bullshit! Where are they?"

"He . . . doesn't . . . "

"The fuck he doesn't! Where are they?"

She sighed uncomfortably. "He . . . "

"Dammit bitch!" Tony slugged Phillip in the face hard enough to knock the kid out of consciousness. "WHERE ARE THEY?"

Sue screamed hysterically, not only for her child, but due to the pain of her restraint as well. Her eyes were shut as tight as a newborn's, face glossy with an outpour of tears that seemed to have no end.

"What?" was all she could get out through sobs of grief.

Randy screamed for her head, but Tony blocked his tirade. "Dan's guns. Where are they?" he said calmly.

She looked into his eyes through her own gagging restraint. She could see his motives, but his eyes did not speak for Randy.

"I just need to be in control of this house, that's all," said Tony. "I have no intentions of using a gun. I just need to know where Dan's weapons are,"

Besides.

"Besides."

If you don't tell me.

"If you don't tell me."

I'm gonna have to carve little Phil here like a turkey.

"I'm gonna have to carve little Phil here like a turkey."

"Noooooooo!"

Tony was appalled at what he had said, but how different was it from everything else he had said and done today?

"Computer room, behind the picture on the wall," she sobbed. "The combination is . . . seven . . . twenty-four . . . fifteen."

"You may have just saved your son's life."

Where did that come from? He had no intention of harming the boy any worse than a bloodied nose or a punch to the gut here and there to illustrate a point, or in a case such as this one: to acquire information.

Tony left the desperate atmosphere of Phillip's room, and then checked the doors of the hallway until he found the computer room. Indeed there was a painting on the wall. Once removed, it revealed a hidden safe. The safe wasn't very large, not big enough to store a shotgun or rifle, but plenty big for a handgun.

Sure enough, there was a revolver and a pistol with ammunition to spare. Along with the guns and ammo were the titles to their vehicles, three birth certificates and a stack of documents likely pertaining to the house and other such investments.

All Tony wanted was the guns.

Chapter 14
A promise to keep

"All right!" said Tony. "Up and at 'em! We're moving the show into the master bedroom. There's something I want Dan to see."

He startled the duo as he jumped into the bedroom from the hallway spouting off orders. Tony grabbed one of the knots in the rope that restrained Phillip and began untying it.

"Get up, Sue. I've got a promise I have to keep with your husband."

"I . . . I can't get—"

"Sure you can. You just have to try."

With her arms stretched behind her back it was difficult to balance herself and stand without falling to either side. She tried twice and failed. Falling caused a reflexive action for Sue to put her hands out to break the fall, but she couldn't. This reflex caused Sue more pain in her cramped muscles and from the rope burn on her neck than it did in the actual fall.

"Try again, honey, you can do it."

Tony stopped what he was doing for a moment and thought about what he had just said, about what he was doing. He was allowing this woman not only to be restrained in a severely torturous fashion, but forcing her to stand up knowing damn well she was going to fall a few times. And what was with calling her honey? That was something Randy would have said.

"Forget about it, fuck it. Gotta move on." Tony mumbled as he untied the last of the rope from the bed.

"Okay, Phil, don't try anything smart or I'll bust you in the face again. Deal?"

Phillip nodded.

"Good."

* * *

As Tony used some of the same rope to bind his hands

around his back, Phillip noticed the two guns tucked into his belt on either hip like some half-cocked gunslinger. The ammunition made a rectangular bulge in his pockets.

That was the first real moment Phillip thought he was going to die.

"Okay, troops," Tony said, "walk in a single file line through the hallway into the master bedroom. As you can see," he pulled out the pistol, "I have a gun and it's loaded and pointed at your head. Don't try to be a hero, either of you. Let's move."

"Go ahead, Phillip," Sue said, her voice quivering.

Phillip was beyond crying. He cried all the tears he had in him and there just weren't any left. He had to be a man, and so he took the lead and walked through the door into the hallway where he turned left toward the master bedroom. At least being in front he didn't have to see his mother in so much pain.

If only he could get free and take the guns away from Tony, what pain he would make that man feel. Phillip wasn't old enough to truly understand anger, but a situation such as this one made men of mere boys.

It wasn't how it was supposed to be, but the terrible scene that was unfolding was making a man out of Phillip. He would have been a child for several more years, never knowing despair, true fear, survival or hatred, and then only slowly, learning these monumental feelings would have caused his manhood to break free from his adolescent cocoon.

He understood love as well. The love for his family, a love that would have slowly dawned on him as he grew older, and eventually as his parents grew old and frail he would have known completely as a wise man. But he was nothing more than a child learning of things no child should have to.

His father was tied to the bed. Phillip didn't quite understand alcohol, but he knew what it was and knew what it made his father become. The room smelt faintly of the stuff and Phillip couldn't help but wonder if that made it easier for Tony to tie his father up, sick as he always was the day after drinking.

For such a young boy he certainly knew logic and deduction.

* * *

"Against the wall, both of you," Tony ordered.

94

When Sue hobbled into the room, Dan went ballistic. His eyes popped out of his head, veins bulging around his neck like a body builder attempting maximum weight. He screamed and cursed inaudible words spitting saliva and blood from his mess of a mouth. Though it was hard to discern his vocalizations, expletives were prevalent.

"Dan," Tony said calmly as he pulled the pistol from his belt. "Remember what I told you."

Dan shut up very quickly.

"How the fuck did you find them?" Dan looked to his wife as he liquidly said these words. There was really only one way Tony could have gotten into the safe.

"Yeah, I told you, you should have let me know where they were. I thought of you as a hunter, a real woodsy lumberjack type, but I guess I was wrong." Tony pulled the revolver out of his belt holding the mismatched guns like a Wild West gunfighter.

"What do you have them for, Dan? Not for survival, they wouldn't have been stashed in the safe if they were for survival. Hell, you could have had one stored away under your mattress and pulled it on me earlier." Tony paused. "Probably not, though. I would have put a knife in your gut first."

Go with the flow, little bro.

Tony's eyes went blank. He hadn't heard Randy say that since they were teenagers living in San Diego, California. How could that fuck of a brother of his infiltrate his mind this way? It was enough to make a man crazy.

"Don't answer, don't you fucking answer," Tony said to no one in particular, at least no one that could be seen in the room.

Even in the excruciating pain Sue's muscles and bent neck were causing her, it was apparent that there was something very wrong with Tony's mental health, something beyond his violence toward the Ritters.

Dan stared from the bed, witness to Tony's madness. He had his own episodes of insanity, one only last night. In some sick way he could relate to Tony, to the struggle that was playing within his mind, though he felt no sympathy for the mad bastard.

Both Sue and Dan were wrong in their convictions about Tony's behavior. Sure, he may have been acting out slightly more sadistic than he normally would have in such a situation, but that didn't mean Randy's voice of insanity was causing him to take this family hostage.

He had to take them hostage regardless of Randy's blather, for other reasons.

"You remember what I told you, right, Dan? About finding the guns. How I was going to kill your family in front of your eyes slow and methodically." Tony's calm voice turned into blind rage. "You remember that, Dan!"

Sue cried, huddling up to her son who was trying to see what was happening, trying to assess the situation.

"You wouldn't." Dan shook his head in disbelief.

"No. I wont. That wouldn't do me a lick of good. I don't have to worry about them; it's you I'm worried about. Your boy, your wife—who fucking cares, man, but you . . . you're a danger to me." Tony holstered the pistol, and then took the revolver in his right hand pointing it at Dan's head.

"I think your punishment for not telling me where the guns were should be worse than you watching your family die, 'cause frankly I'm not sure they mean a whole hell of a lot to you anyhow. They, on the other hand, look up to you even though you're a hapless alcoholic, so I think it is only just that they watch you die slowly because of your mistake."

"Noooooo!" Sue screamed in tears, her voice hoarse.

Tony looked at Sue and Phillip clutched together on the ground. He realized just how much the boy looked like his father in the eyes. If his old man were without a beard they would look even more alike.

The kid wasn't crying. *Why?* After all this, the little shit looked headstrong and furious. *By God, the little fuck wants me dead*, Tony thought.

Make him cry, Randy added, and for the first time Tony didn't mind Randy's commentary. *Make the little fucker cry, man. Make him feel weak.*

Up to now the revolver had been pointed at Dan's head. Tony lowered the gun and shot Dan in the leg just below the kneecap. The sound was deafening.

The wound wasn't clean, but rather a small explosion of flesh and cartilage from Dan's shin. Sue screamed hysterically, Dan screamed in pain; Phillip looked shocked though his death-stare on Tony faltered none.

"How do you like that, Phil? You like that well? How do you

like this?" Tony pointed the gun at Dan's wrist, pulled the trigger sending the bullet into the mattress and inch away from Dan's arm. Sue screamed again at the sound of the gun, eyes closed to the carnage before her.

"I missed," Tony said dully.

Phillip's eyes widened a bit. It was a point for his team, but this wasn't a game and points could be wiped off the board with one bullet.

Shoot his nose off, man. Do something that'll really fuck with the kid.

Neither hesitation nor scorn delayed Tony from his movement to the head of the bed. He knelt down facing Dan's profile. What a mess Dan looked with his torn lip and bloodied beard, shivering in a combination of fear and shock. Tony grabbed Dan by the throat with his free hand holding his head reasonably steady as he shoved the revolver into the side of his nose.

He did just as Randy suggested and blew Dan's nose off in a wild mist of blood. The bullet flew across the room lodging itself through the mirrored closet door into the plaster closet wall. Dan's face was now a spectacle of disgust. His upper lip and nose were nothing more than a crater of singed, ripped, blood-oozing flesh. His screams were piercing and more than Tony could handle.

"Shut up!" Tony screamed.

But Dan wouldn't shut up—he couldn't shut up. Half his face was blown into microscopic bits and he was supposed to shut up? It was impossible.

"How do you like that?" Tony said, retreating to the bathroom where he could collect his thoughts on what he had done.

There were screams in the bedroom, maybe worse than he had ever heard in his tainted past with Randy, a past he thought he had left in the past. He never wanted to take hostages ever again after Randy died, but in this situation, it seemed like there was no other choice.

Sue had recognized him, after all.

And that wasn't a good thing.

He simply could not have loose ends.

Dan was going to die and there was no question about that. Why Tony was doing it in such a slow torturous fashion, he wasn't entirely sure. It was something his brother would have done for sure, but he . . .

Never . . . until this snowy meeting.

Maybe it was cabin fever. Maybe he was losing his mind with the knowledge that he was going to be locked in this foreign house for a day or two with a family of strangers, of which the mother recognized him as the man from the bank. The *bank*!

What dumb luck. He knew at that moment when she made her knowledge of him clear that there was going to be trouble.

Of all the houses, I had to pick this one, he thought.

You know what you gotta do, bro, you gotta wipe 'em all out. You gotta wipe 'em all out and make a getaway that the snow will cover. You can't just kill him. She was the one who recognized you.

Randy had a point. Dan didn't know him from a hole in the ground, but Sue . . . she was the one that would recognize his face. She was the one who would see him on the news and be able to call the police and give them a lead.

The police! What am I thinking?

Sitting on the toilet with the lid down, Tony thought about what he had gotten himself into. With the snow storm the police wouldn't even be looking for him for several days. They may not be looking for him at all, but being a man of sin and a sordid past he felt that the police were always hot on his trail when he did something illegal, and when he did something illegal it was usually a heavy felony.

In the past he never dealt dime bags and quarter ounces of drugs, he sold it in pounds and kilos; never roughed a guy up, he killed him; didn't just steal a car, he stole a fleet of cars.

And as he was now with the voice of his departed brother he was then with the real thing. As much as he tried to get his shit together, old habits really did die hard. And when old habits could get you twenty to life, they died the hardest.

If you're not going to kill the kid then you better put the fear of God into him.

"But I'm not you, Randy. You were the one to fuck with people like this."

Tony looked through the bathroom door to the mess of a man on the bed and his tortured family across the room. Sue was half mad but her son was strangely sober, staring into Tony's eyes.

How do you think we got through it, man? If it wasn't for me. . .

Whether there was truth to what Randy's voice said, Tony

didn't know. In some ways, Randy was right, but if it wasn't for Randy's psychotic behaviors, he may be alive today.

That was a different story altogether and you know it. This is just a place to hide out the storm, and a family that doesn't mean shit to you. If they live you'll be wanted and won't make it through the snow and out of Colorado.

"Christ you make sense sometimes."

Tony opened the medicine cabinet searching for something he could use. "The fear of God," he mumbled fingering through cotton balls and Band-Aids, toothpaste and tampons.

He decided on shaving razors.

"This is for you, Phil, looking at me like a robot. You want to see what you're doing to your father, staring at me like that."

"Don't do anything else to him," Phillip pleaded. "You're hurting him, you're killing him."

"Not me, son. You're the one who's mad-doggin' me. You're killing him."

Phillip averted his attention thinking that maybe Tony would have mercy on his father.

"Look at me, boy," Tony said. "Look at your father."

Tony dragged the shaving razor over Dan's body in a motion like shaving hair, only he was applying pressure, causing thin shavings of Dan's flesh to curl from the blade like bloody red pencil shavings. Tony didn't have to look at Phillip to know he was watching—he could hear the boy sobbing.

The room was agony, the sounds of a family in horror crying together. Sobs and whining like ghosts in old tales.

Dan was a bloody mess from head to toe. That he hadn't passed out from sheer exhaustion and pain was miraculous; that he hadn't passed out from loss of blood—alcohol thinned blood—was proof of his want to protect his family. Perhaps he wasn't as heartless as Tony thought.

"We've got to clean this man up," Tony said grabbing the bottle of rubbing alcohol from the nightstand. "Don't want those cuts to get infected, now do we." He poured the alcohol over Dan's body, the clear liquid revealing the swatches of raw flesh that seemed to bleed just as quickly as the alcohol washed it away. Dan's screams were hoarse and frantic, his body now convulsing on the blood and sweat soaked bed.

"This is a message to both of you." Tony stood at the headboard holding the revolver. "Don't fuck with me. Dan fucked with me. He neglected to tell me what I needed to know and this is what happened to him. Remember this when you think about double-crossing me, when you think about fucking me, when you think about escaping me. Think of this." Tony pointed the gun at Dan's head and discharged the fatal shot. Dan's screaming ceased immediately, quieting the room save that of the storm outside and Sue's frantic whimpers.

Chapter 15
Look what you did!

On the T.V. was an old re-run of Gilligan's Island. Tony was laughing hysterically at the primitive humor as he cooked fried eggs and toast in the kitchen. Sue and Phil were seated on the couch in front of the TV, neither of them laughing or hungry. Sue was finally free from her arm and back straining bind and sitting with her arms around her legs, knees up to her chin. Her hands and feet were tied together. Phillip was in a less restrictive restraint with his feet and hands tied together by a chain that connected the two much like a death row inmate.

It was mid-afternoon, an hour after Dan met his maker, and no, Sue and her son were not hungry. But Tony was insistent. He told them they must eat and be happy to have been freed from their oppressor.

But Tony didn't know Dan. Dan wasn't a nightly drunk, never laid a hand on either his wife or son. He had suffered from a mental problem that only he and his late father knew about, and when those issues arose, alcohol was the magic cure. It just so happened that Tony took refuge with the Ritters on one of his problem nights.

The laughing in the kitchen stopped. It had been damn near constant ever since Tony turned on the TV, and now that it ceased, something was wrong. At least with the laughter, Sue and Phil knew where and what Tony was doing—it made him seem less angry.

Sue turned her head, eyes fearing what she would see, perhaps a pistol pointed in her direction or maybe a steak knife ready for her eye, but what she saw was not immediately dangerous yet terribly frightening.

Tony hovered over the frying eggs, spatula in hand. The eggs were popping in the pan, asking to be flipped. Yet he stood there, eyes wide, mumbling to himself.

Sue turned to her son who was also staring at Tony. "He's mad," she whispered. "I think he lost it."

The toast was burning. Tendrils of smoke escaped the toaster oven. It was the smell of burning toast that pulled Tony from his trance.

"Oh shit! Burnt the fucking toast!" He opened the glass door to the toaster oven and pulled the rack out with an oven-mitt, then slammed the toast into the sink as if it were going to bite him. He flipped his eggs realizing that he had burnt them as well. An egg flew across the room toward the T.V. He went into a mild tirade slamming utensils and pans about cursing himself for burning their afternoon breakfast.

"Looks like breakfast is out," Tony said as he walked past his prisoners and down the hall to the master bedroom.

"Dammit Randy! Look what you did," Tony's voice echoed from the bedroom as he rediscovered Dan's mutilated body on the bed. "You fucking junkie! I leave you alone for one second and you cut the guy into ribbons."

In the living room, Phillip and his mother looked at each other scared as to what may happen next. They were listening to a man's mind cracking up one piece at a time. Tony sounded like a schizophrenic talking to some imaginary fiend named Randy. After what they watched him do to Dan there was no telling what he was capable of. Insanity wasn't predictable.

"Where are you? Listen to me! You gotta help me with this one. Help me clean this shit up."

Tony reentered the living room. "Where are . . . " his eyes caught sight of Phillip and Sue on the couch. He didn't recognize them, which was apparent as he looked around the room cautiously.

"Where is he?" Tony finally asked. "Where's my brother."

"Randy?" Sue said.

"So he *is* here . . . " Tony was scared as he searched the room for his dead brother. "He must have..."

"He didn't do anything. No one else is here," said Sue. "You k-killed..." she began sobbing again. "M-m-m-my husband."

"I didn't kill him. It was that brother of mine, Randy."

"There is no Randy!" she screamed. "There's no one else here but us!"

Hey, whoa. Calm down, man. You're flyin' off the deep end here.

"Randy?"

Dude, I had to take control for a second there, you were

gonna chicken out, man. You gotta get back into your head, man; remember what's goin' on here. You had to kill her old man. He was your only real threat, but remember what I said. You have to kill her, too. She recognizes you from the bank.

"Oh, my God," Tony said grabbing his head. "I'm losing my fucking mind."

Do the smart thing and kill the both of them. Just wait the storm out and get to Canada.

"Shut up." Tony said these words under his breath, barely moving his lips. Sweat poured down his face profusely, his heartbeat racing. "Shut up."

I didn't know you would flip out if I took control, man, but I don't know if you can do this by yourself.

"Shut up!"

Sue and Phillip winced, half expecting to be hit, shot or stabbed at any moment.

"Just shut up and leave me alone. You've caused me enough trouble in the past and now there's a fucking bloody-ass corpse and I need you to just get the fuck out of my head and just leave me the fuck alone," his voice rose. "BEFORE I LOSE MY FUCKING MIND!"

Chapter 16
There are no should haves

Outside, the storm peaked leaving the driveway, SR 54 and everything else buried under several feet of snow. The wind softened a bit, floating flakes of ice through the air like a child's dream of Christmas morning. Icicles hung from the eaves like stalactites or the teeth of an ice monster. It was a beautiful sight from the windows of every other house along SR 54, but for Tony it was a dreadful reminder of the time he was going to have to wait until he could shovel the driveway and leave this house and its miserable inhabitants.

Tony didn't wish harm to them, but he knew Sue was going to have to die. He watched the snowflakes fall softly, the way snow was portrayed in movies, drifting with the wind hither and thither, when he realized the dire situation he had made for himself. Well, Randy had a hand—from beyond the grave—in the matter. Just like old times, Randy had managed to take a simple hostage situation and turn it into a frenzied blood bath.

Tony should have known better, should have left work earlier to get as far ahead of the snow as possible, should have risked the cold in his car; he should have dismissed his life of crime with Randy's body back in Ohio.

There are no should haves, and now is no time for fucking around, Tony thought. It was his own mental voice this time.

Tony turned from the window he had been staring from to see Sue and her son on the couch. They weren't facing him, but rather in a sort of praying posture, their faces pale and waxen.

It should have been easy to kill them, but it wasn't. Tony wasn't much of a killer. Brutal he could be, but killer . . . that was Randy's forte, getting screwed up and harming innocent people. That was why Randy took control of Tony's body and did Dan in.

Phillip and Sue were innocent, after all. What had they done? They had been kind to a perfect stranger and what did it get them? A dead husband/father and a pair of completely wrecked minds, that's what.

Tony pulled the revolver from his waistband pointing it at his captives. They were completely oblivious of his gesture. *Are they praying*? Perhaps.

His finger curled around the trigger. All it would take is an eighth of an inch of movement from his pointer finger and the bullet would jet from the barrel into Sue's head.

What was he waiting for, the whisper from his late brother telling him it was all right to blow her brains out?

You're on your own, bro.

Tony squeezed the trigger. The bullet flew through the air faster than the blink of an eye entering the back of Sue's head blowing an ugly hole as it exited via her face.

Phillip screamed, jumping back in pure instinctual reaction. His mother's body hit the floor face down, the white carpet quickly turning red around her destroyed face. Phillip continued screaming and yelling hysterically.

"Shut up, kid!" Tony yelled. The barrel of his gun was pointed in Phillip's direction. "There's nothing you can do about it, kid. If you try anything stupid I'll blow your fucking head off, and I think you've seen proof of that."

"You asshole! You . . . you . . . " Phillip began sobbing. "You killed my mom . . . asshole!"

Tony walked across the room and backhanded Phil's face as hard as he could. Phillip was silenced, staring at his captor. He brought both of his chained hands to comfort his burning cheek. The red outline of Tony's hand was becoming clear as the blood flushed Phil's face.

"Thought that'd shut you up. You don't have to die you know. If you stick with me until SR 54 is plowed, you can live to see another day. As for your folks...lets just say it's too bad your mother recognized me and your father was a hapless drunk."

"He wasn't a drunk," Phillip contradicted, looking everywhere except the floor where his mother's body lay.

Tony slapped Phillip again hard enough to dislocate his jaw, but the kid had good, strong bones thus his jaw stayed intact merely aching. "That's not a good way to start surviving, Phil. Talking back can result in a busted jaw." Tony looked at him like a father to a son. "Just do what I say and talk when spoken to, and you'll be home free. Got it?"

Phillip dared a look at his mother's corpse, shivering at the sight. As the saying goes, mothers and fathers shouldn't live to see their children die. The same is true in the case of young children seeing their mothers and fathers die.

"Got it!" Tony Yelled.

Phillip nodded his head, sobbing.

"Now, I want you to follow me everywhere I go. If I see that you're not following me, I will hurt you. It's as simple as that. I need to know where you are at all times. You got that?"

Phillip was reluctant to answer. It wasn't that he didn't hear Tony, but rather that he was in shock. To lay unreasonable orders on a boy's head after shooting his mother was cruel. How could Tony expect Phil to answer?

Though Tony was a hardened criminal (removed from the life of crime up until recently), he did have a heart and found it painful to watch the boy sulking over his parents' deaths.

"Phillip, c'mon, follow me," Tony said as he headed for the hallway. Phillip didn't move. "Hey!" Phillip looked up suddenly, startled from his mournful daze. "You've got to follow me. I need to know where you are at all times, and later I'm gonna need your help, so come over here."

"You might as well kill me," Phillip said looking at Tony with wide, sad eyes.

"Is that what you think?" Tony raised his eyes. "Maybe you need a little bit of what my father called 'convincing.'"

Tony crossed the room and grabbed Phillip's arm. "When we were out of line my father liked to 'convince' us that what we were doing was wrong, to 'convince' us that we had better behave. I just hope you're not as stupid as my brother was. Sometimes it took him a lot of 'convincing.'"

"Let go of me. I'm sorry, I'll do whatever you say."

"Too late, kid. Ever heard of an African sting bee?"

"No," Phillip sniveled.

Tony pinched a rather large piece of skin on Philip's arm between his pointer finger and thumb getting a good grip then twisted the skin as hard as he could. Phillip screamed in agony then Tony grabbed another bit of his skin and gave him another one a little further up his arm.

"That's an African sting bee."

Tony let go of the boy's arm. Phillip lost his balance tumbling to the ground, his shackles restricting him from breaking the fall with his hands. The bright red African sting bees on his arm were puffing up into welts.

"You mind what I say or there'll be more where that came from, and there's plenty of places you don't want an African sting bee, believe me." Tony stared at the kid for a moment wondering if he was going to cooperate. "Now, follow me."

Tony walked to the hallway, happy to see that Phillip was following him.

Chapter 17
What to do with the bodies

Tony put Phillip back in his room after taking a screwdriver from the garage and reversing the door handle so it would lock from the outside, after which he drilled a hole in the door so he could peek in at Phillip.

"By now you should know not to fuck around and try anything stupid, so just sit tight in here until I need you. Your parents might be dead, but that doesn't mean you have to meet your maker just yet. All you have to do is cooperate."

Tony looked at the kid with empathy. "Maybe try and get some sleep, you look like hell," he said before shutting the door and locking it on the outside. The kid had been through hell in the past twenty-four hours, a hell no child should ever have to experience, and it wasn't over. For now, Tony was in control, but there was no way of knowing when he was going to lose it again and torture Phillip the way he did his father.

What to do with the bodies, Tony mused. They were both a filthy and disgusting mess, especially Dan, but he was on a bed, which may be a small blessing as far as clean up was concerned. Sue, on the other hand, was lying on the living room floor (the *white* living room floor) bleeding clear into the foundation by now. How much blood could come from a headshot of that magnitude? A pint, two at the most.

On the television was a re-run of Bonanza.

What's black and white and red all over? Randy asked inside Tony's head. *An episode of Bonanza on a TV covered in blood.*

Very funny, Tony thought. He could see that even after death Randy hadn't lost his morbid sense of humor.

The television console was blasted with brain and skull matter along with the wall behind it. Cleaning all that was ridiculous. There was really no way for Tony to cover his tracks completely. He had made two huge messes in this house and that was that. He would be long gone before anyone found out about this place anyway, and there won't be anyone left who could recognize him.

Phillip will recognize you, bro. You need to pop the kid, too.

"Fuck you, Randy. It's that kind of thinking that got you killed in the first place. It's that kind of thinking that led me to killing his fucking parents. You son-of-a-bitch. If it wasn't for you they would all be tied up and alive."

That kid'll remember your name. You don't want that, man.

"Shut up. Fuck off!"

Tony stormed down the hallway, passed Phillip's room and headed for the master bedroom. Furiously, he began pulling the sheets off the bed, wrapping them around Dan's body.

Taking the duct tape he had used earlier, he stuck it on the sheet then attempted to roll the body as to wrap it in duct tape. Dan was a big 'ole boy weighing in at least two hundred and fifty pounds, and when he rolled he toppled off the bed thumping on the floor like the pile of dead meat that he was. On the floor, Tony tried to roll his body carefully as not to touch the coagulated-blood soaked bottom of the sheets.

He had no luck taping Dan up so he decided to wrap tape around Dan's head and feet securing the blanket that way.

From there, Tony went into the room where he slept the first night and pulled the linens from the bed. He brought the sheets and blanket into the living room and wrapped Sue in them. Her body was considerably easier to deal with being that she weighed a fraction of what her husband did. He successfully wrapped her body in duct tape from head to toe in a nice tight bundle (what he had attempted to do with Dan).

As for the byproduct of his violence—the blood and gore that littered the bed and the wall in the master bedroom and the splattered television console in the living room—Tony could care less. If anything, he would put Phillip on splatter duty.

In the garage Tony found gloves, a good thick jacket, and a snow shovel.

Outside, the storm was at a lull for the first time in over twenty-four hours; however, there was no sign of the sun, which meant the snow and ice would sit dormant in the cold winter air.

Shovel in hand, Tony walked through the house to a sliding glass door that led to a patio at the mouth of the backyard. He originally wanted Phillip to do the shoveling, but decided it would be too strenuous for him. The last thing Tony wanted was for Phil to freeze to death before he had a chance to help carry the bodies outside.

Tony opened the sliding glass door. A gust of chilled air blew into the house, the first chill he had felt since he was on the front porch talking to the lumberjack of a man he came to briefly know as Dan. It didn't feel good, but what had to be done had to be done, regardless of the chill.

The snow was at least three feet thick, maybe four, which disguised the landscape of the backyard. This could be tricky. If there was an abrupt slope Tony would be oblivious to it and risk sliding down the hill. On the other hand, by the look of the trees there was little possibility of a slope. There could be a ditch, or even a compost hole, but that was a risk he was going to have to take.

Without further ado, Tony used the snow shovel and began blazing a trail through the snow. It was hard work but would be worth doing in the long run.

After what seemed like an hour, Tony decided he had trailed far enough. He cleared a large space (large enough for two adult bodies) then walked back to the house where he had left a spade shovel. He took the spade shovel and tried to dig two shallow graves. The earth was frozen and far too hard to dig into. Burying them under the snow would at least make it a little more difficult for the police to find the bodies, at least until the thaw.

The warmth in the house was like a good hot cup of coffee—Tony had cranked the heat after taking control. When he entered the house as the storm was in its infancy he never would have thought that he was going to be burying two bodies in this retched weather. Of course, back when he used to run around with his crazy brother he would have expected anything. Burying two bodies in the snow was ginger beer compared to what mayhem Randy would have gotten them into.

But didn't Randy get me into this raw deal, Tony thought. *Technically, wasn't it his idea to knock off the whole family?*

Regardless, Randy was dead which automatically handed over any responsibility to Tony. There was no scapegoat, at least outside of Tony's tortured mind.

At least I'm in control now, Tony thought.

Dressed in a heavy jacket and gloves, Tony opened the door to Phillip's room. The sudden intrusion startled the boy.

"I'm going to need your help, kid." Tony walked into the room. "I'm going to undo your hand and ankle cuffs. I think you're smart enough to do what I ask." Tony took the key from his key ring and began unlatching the all too real costume handcuffs.

"I'm bigger and stronger than you, too. Keep that in mind if you think about getting away. If you thought those African sting bees hurt, you've got another thing coming."

With the boy unshackled Tony said, "Now, get long-johns and a thermal undershirt on and some good winter clothes. We're going outside for a little while."

Phillip looked at him bashfully. "Do you think you can wait in the hall?" he asked timidly.

"No can do, pal, we're both men here. Change your clothes and make it quick, and no funny stuff."

Without trying his luck with stubborn persistence, Phillip began dressing for the snow. That little boy's shyness of dressing in front of a stranger was perhaps the final act of childishness Phillip would ever have.

In a few minutes, they were in the master bedroom hovering over the large bundle on the floor formerly known as Dan. Phillip knew the bundle was his father and choked back tears. If he were to be able to get through this, he was going to have to get tough.

Tony looked Phil in the eyes. "He's heavy. We're going to have to lift him and carry him through the back door." Tony reached down and grabbed the shroud by the shoulders. "You take the legs, they're lighter."

Reluctantly, Phillip kneeled down and grabbed his father's legs. Feeling weak in the knees, he wasn't sure how he was going to carry the body all the way down the hall and out the sliding glass door to the backyard, not to mention across the small path Tony plowed to the burial site.

"On three," said Tony. "One . . . two . . . three!"

Tony hefted his side of the blood soiled, blanket-wrapped body as much as he could. Phillip lifted the legs, which was only a fraction of Dan's dead weight. They tried to move the body but it was dragging along the ground by the midsection and Tony certainly didn't want a trail of blood leading to Dan's whereabouts.

"This isn't working. Drop it," Tony said.

Tony thought for a moment. "Do you have a skateboard?" he asked.

Phillip nodded his head.

"Where is it? The garage?"

Phillip nodded his head again. He was in no mood for talking. The act of discarding his father's corpse depressed his already melancholy state.

"Follow me," Tony said exiting the bedroom.

There were two skateboards in the garage to Tony's surprise. He wasn't sure one would support Dan's weight, but two would work just fine.

They walked back to the master bedroom, each holding a skateboard. Phillip gripped his with white knuckled fists wanting so badly to lift the wheeled board of wood and smash it into Tony's head. He couldn't though. Likely, he wouldn't have the strength to knock the man out which would have the same result as poking a sleeping bear with a stick.

As much as Phil tried to construct a plan against Tony, he was shit out of luck. Now that his hands and feet were free from the chains and handcuffs, he was at better liberty to get away, but where to? The snow was almost as tall as he was and running through it would be a certain prescription for hypothermia, and where would he run? The nearest neighbor was at least a half a mile down SR 54.

"All right, Phil," Tony said as he grabbed the legs of the bloodied shroud. "I'm going to lift him and I want you to slide the skateboards under him one at a time next to each other. They'll support his midsection so we can wheel him down the hall to the back yard."

Phillip nodded his head. It felt wholly wrong to be sliding skateboards under his father's rump. The whole idea of dragging his body outside was bad enough.

Tony lifted the legs of the body. "Okay, Phil, slide them under."

Phillip did as he was told, carefully as not to get any of his father's blood on his clothes.

Tony let the legs down walking to the other side of the corpse grabbing and lifting the shoulders as he had done before.

"Grab the legs, boy, we're going to haul him to the back yard."

Phillip grabbed the legs and they hauled him off. The skateboard idea worked like a charm, Dan's dead weight applying enough pressure so the boards didn't want to go off in their own directions. They skated him down the hallway and had a little trouble pushing the skateboard across the living room carpet as the wheels wanted to dig in.

Outside, the skateboard was useless. As much as Tony wanted Phil to help him, he grabbed the legs of the cadaver and hauled it himself down the icy path he had shoveled an hour ago.

"One more," Tony said as he passed Phillip. "Follow me," he said, not looking back. "From now on I want you to follow me wherever I go unless I say otherwise, got it?"

Phillip nodded.

"Makes things easier for the both of us," Tony muttered.

Treatin' the kid like he's actually going to live. Nice touch, Randy piped in. Tony looked at Phillip wondering for a split second if he could hear the awful chorus of his late brother's rambling voice. Phillip's expressionless stare remained unchanged. Randy was still a figment locked inside Tony's mind like a personal torture device.

After he helps you carry his mom out there you're gonna shoot him and bury him with them, aren't you?

"She's much lighter, grab her legs," Tony said disregarding his brother's psychosis.

There was something in Tony's eyes, something that had been there in the bedroom while he butchered Dan. Something Phil decided to call: The Madness.

They carried Sue's sheet-wrapped body through the snow path and dropped it next to the bundle that was his father.

"Take this shovel and start piling snow on them," Tony said handing Phil the spade shovel.

Phillip was calm and responsive. He started shoveling snow without hesitation. This part of the process was easier for him. He convinced himself that he was laying his mother and father to rest, however absurd it was.

As they walked back to the house, Tony used the snow shovel to cover their tracks, attempting to make it look as if no one had trekked through the backyard.

Phillip had half a mind to smash Tony's face with the spade shovel. It would be easy enough to do, and if he wanted to, he could use the shovel as a blade and decapitate the son-of-a-bitch. Once again, he wasn't confident. Tony was a dangerous man and very intimidating. He had a perpetual look of mistrust and anger on his rough sandpaper face. His jet black hair made him all the more evil looking, like a grown up bully.

"Don't even think it, boy," Tony said. He could see something brewing in Phillip's mind. "I've been watching you with that shovel, don't think I haven't. You would be damn foolish to try and swat me with it."

Phillip shook his head from side to side wide-eyed and frightened. "I . . . I wasn't . . . " the kid was at a loss for words.

"That's what I thought," Tony said with a sardonic grin. "You were thinking it though, I know that, could see it in your eyes."

Tony walked back into the house. He knew Phillip would be right behind him. "I better not see that in your eyes again," Tony said with his back to Phil. "Now, put that shovel back in the garage."

"Yes, sir."

I like that, Tony thought. *I could get used to being called sir.*

You fucked up, bro. Why didn't you knock him off and bury him with his parents? Are you crazy?

"Maybe."

He'll recognize you. Your fingerprints are all over this place. You have to get rid of him.

Tony didn't respond. He was trying to ignore his dead-beat brother's bad advice. He figured that maybe if he ignored the voice in his head it would go away.

Phillip came back in the house.

"Have a seat in the kitchen. I'll make us some dinner."

Apprehensively, Phillip took a seat.

Chapter 18
A bite, a drink, and sleep

They had dinner: macaroni and cheese—the cheap knock off brand with the orange powder—and a couple of hamburger patties with ketchup. Phillip wasn't hungry, but the smell of hamburger made his mouth water, not to mention his love for mac and cheese.

They ate, watched TV, and in no time, Phillip was out cold. Earlier, when he had went to use the bathroom, Tony ground up a few sleeping pills and added it to his Kool-Aid.

Tony picked the boy up like an oversized baby and took him into the living room where he set him down on the love seat.

Awww, pudding duh baby do bed, Randy mimed. *You're a real tool, Tony. You ought to stick a pillow over the kid's face and get it over with.*

Tony ignored the annoying voice and proceeded with what he was doing. Randy must be ignored, that was the only way to get through this without any further bloodshed. Tony was in far too deep as it was.

Knowing the dose of grounded up sleeping pills would have Phillip out all night, Tony decided against restraining the boy. As for himself, he watched the eleven o'clock news. Tomorrow morning the plows would be on the roads along with the first sign of sunlight in several days.

This was what Tony had been waiting for. His stay was finally drawing to an end. When he slid his car into the driveway, nearly creaming Dan's truck in the process, he never thought it would end up in a double homicide. If anything, he would have hogtied the family in the living room and left it at that.

If it wasn't for Randy.

"Randy," he whispered. "You son-of-a-whore, Randy. Even now you're screwing things up. What, are you pissed off that I didn't get shot and killed with you, that I was smart enough to get the fuck out before the cops arrived?"

There was no answer from the Randy-voice in his mind, the

115

Randy-voice that he so much hated, the voice that spoke to him beyond his control. A ghost perhaps. It was more like having an invader that he could actually converse with right up there in his own noggin. Some people would call that insanity.

It had to be his own imagination, but there was something so real about Randy's voice. That was the most frightening part. Tony tried to convince himself that it was the stress getting to him, yet it was more than that. He was losing himself, wasn't he?

He remembered what Randy had said: 'I had to take control for a second there. You were gonna chicken out, man.'

Take control! What the fuck did that mean? Tony Wondered. Was there a period when he wasn't in control of his facilities? Imaginations didn't usually take control. At least Tony didn't think they did.

Either way, it changed nothing. If he could manage to ignore Randy's bloviating and get away from the house without harming Phillip, everything would be all right.

He just hoped Randy would leave him alone. After all was said and done and he made it across the border into Canada, the last thing he wanted was to have to live with his brother trapped inside his mind. Whether he was a ghost or stress-induced imagination, that would be enough to drive anyone crazy.

On that note, Tony decided to go to sleep. He had a long day of shoveling the driveway ahead of him.

Chapter 19
Day three: sunshine and snowplows

Tony woke with the foreign rays of sunshine gleaming through the eastern windows. He had purposefully left the drapes open as to allow the expected morning sun into the house. The storm had been brutal and quick. Tony was happy to see it go.

Phillip, out cold on the love seat, lay in a position hardly changed from the night before. Tony checked the boy's pulse. He was still alive. He waited for a smart-ass remark from the uncontrollable taunt of Randy's voice, but none came.

"Good," Tony muttered.

He slipped a handcuff around Phillip's arm that dangled over the loveseat, and clasped the other end to the lamp on the end table. It wouldn't restrain the boy, but it sure would make it impossible for him to make a silent getaway, and probably when he woke he would jerk the lamp to the floor inadvertently.

Coffee would have sounded great on any other cold winter morning, but on this particular morning Tony was pressed for time and work was aplenty. The driveway was huge, and with four feet of snow it was no small feat in shoveling a clear path large enough for a car.

He considered the possibility of using Phillip, but decided to play it safe. The boy might get anxious and try to lay him out with a good smash to the back of the head. Now that his fate was close enough to taste, Tony decided to do the rest by himself and leave Phillip be.

Outside, the chill was deceptive in the light of the sun. The wind factor made the air feel at least ten degrees colder than it really was, but that was nothing Tony wasn't used to. He had shoveled his share of driveways in the past and knew from experience that, sooner than later, he would be sweating and rethinking his reluctance to have Phillip help him.

Tony decided first to locate his car. He had half a mind to use one of their cars, but that would prove more laborious having to transfer the contents from his car to one of theirs, and eventually there would be an APB for the vehicle after the bodies were found, an APB that would include the bordering Canadian cities *and* Mexico.

Being that they owned large trucks, what appeared to be large trucks under the layer of snow when Tony slid into the driveway a few days ago, he decided to shovel snow away from the smallest vehicle and wasn't surprised to see the familiar bumper sticker that read THINK! and for a moment there, he did think.

"What the fuck does *that* mean?"

He hadn't put the sticker on his car. It was there compliments of the prior owner. He was well acquainted with the one word exclamation having seen it every day as he walked to his car from the bank, but until now he had never thought about the beautiful simplicity of the statement.

Tony smiled. He never had been a fan of large gaudy statements and opinions slapped tastelessly on the rear end of motor vehicles, but he liked this one. More people should take the free advice.

Yeah, you ought to take my advice and THINK! about stickin' a pillow over that little shit's face.

"The one person who could have really benefited from such a bumper sticker," Tony said, ignoring Randy's outburst. He took his eyes away from the bumper and began shoveling snow from the car, liberating it from its confinement.

After freeing his car, he began shoveling a path up the driveway and out to the highway, all the while listening to the ranting of Randy.

About thirty minutes after he was finished with the car, Tony had half a mind to use the shovel on himself as to alleviate his mental anguish. At first, it was manageable like listening to a mouthy child who wouldn't stop asking questions, but after a while the cadence and misery of Randy's verbal outpour became intolerable.

The sweat beading his brow and upper lip was half generated from his body heat and half from his accelerating blood pressure. He told himself he was going to ignore the dumb bastard, lock him out, pretend not to hear, but that was impossible. A fly could buzz around one's face ignored only so long before their hand attempted to swat.

"Goddammit, Randy. YOU FUCKING MANIAC!" Tony brought the shovel down on the tail end of his car smashing the left taillight. "Look what you made me do!" This time the shovel came down on the pavement with *clang*. "YOU!" *Clang*! "FUCKING!" *Clang*! "BASTARD!"

After the last word he brought the shovel down as hard as he could hitting a rock which caused the now dented shovel to retract at twice the speed hitting him with the dull edge right between the eyes.

Tony was knocked unconscious. Lying on the half-shoveled driveway, his right eye started puffing, turning black and blue, and his busted nose flowed fresh blood that froze on the icy concrete.

* * *

The first shout woke Phillip abruptly causing him to jerk his outstretched arm, which in turn pulled the lamp to the floor. The boy cringed with the sound of the bulb popping, fearing Tony's reaction to the noise. He closed his eyes tight expecting a gunshot or a knife to slash him, or maybe another arm numbing African sting bee.

He then heard the shouting from outside. Eyes open, the boy strained from his location on the carpet to see over the couch and out the front window where Tony could be heard yelling and slamming something metallic.

Phillip made out the words Randy and bastard. He knew then that The Madness had come over Tony again, which made a strange and frightening situation all the more intense. The Madness made Tony more crazy than he already was, made him do terrible things, made him kill.

Phillip couldn't see very well and didn't want to draw attention to himself. Then, suddenly, the yelling and banging ceased. His heart was a piston, his body tingling with waves of adrenalin. At any moment Tony could walk into the house and point a gun at him with that look in his eyes of no reservations, and what could Phillip do? He was chained to a lamp. Though not an especially heavy lamp, it would slow him down dramatically.

Seconds seemed like minutes, minutes seemed like hours, and nothing. Not a sound.

Phillip noticed for the first time, after his rude awakening, the sun shining through the windows at the front of the house. He then made the correlation. Tony was shoveling the snow. The sound of the banging was probably the snow shovel. That meant he was outside, but that also meant he could be anywhere outside, even the back yard.

Phil gasped; he turned toward the sliding glass door next to the television set expecting fully to see Tony staring in at him with the eyes of The Madness. His heart skipped a beat and he took a deep breath of reassurance at the sight of the vacant sliding glass door.

He looked to the lamp and the cuffs wondering what he could do to un-restrain himself. As long as there was silence he felt he must do something to free himself from the situation. This may be his only chance to get away.

The problem with the lamp was that if he tried to smash it to break himself free, the sound might alert Tony. Alerting Tony to the fact that he was trying to escape would do nothing but get him killed.

He looked around the room, for what he wasn't sure. Then, on the coffee table, Phillip spied a fully loaded key ring. His eyes brightened. The key had to be on that ring.

Cautiously, he inched his way across the rug dragging the broken lamp behind him. The Coffee table was no more than five feet away, but he had to be as quiet as possible. If Tony were to hear him shuffling around and entered the house to find him trying to unlock the handcuffs he would be terminated on the spot, and if his termination was anything like his father's . . .

There was no time for that kind of thinking. Phillip had to move and move fast. This may be his only chance for survival.

Outside, the wind was gentle, irritating a loose gutter. All else was quiet. There was no mad ranting, no banging around. It was almost too quiet for comfort.

Phillip reached the coffee table grabbing the keys like a striking snake. At the sound of the keys jangling, he nearly yelped as he dropped them onto the floor. The carpet muffled the keys metallic shuffle.

Phillip could feel and hear his pulse in his ear, his heart pumping wildly in his chest. He placed a hand over his mouth to stifle his heavy breathing. At that moment he thought Tony would open the front door and discover his little escape plan. He could see the barrel of the gun, the same way his parents had before him. He could imagine the fear they must have felt staring into the barrel.

I can't think about that now, he told himself. Those were the thoughts that could easily paralyze him. There would be plenty of time to mourn his mother and father after he escaped Tony, and getting free from the handcuffs was only part one.

A tear slid down the smooth landscape of Phillip's youthful face. He had thought he was out of tears.

"I have to be tough," he whispered, clenching his teeth in a war grimace.

He thought about the fishing trip with his father last summer. They hiked into the mountains for an hour to get to the hidden lake his father knew about. It was beautiful. There wasn't a soul in sight save that for the occasional deer. They caught several trout, good sized too, and he knew his mother would be happy to cook them up for dinner when they came home, but that never happened.

A hungry bear must have smelled their catch in the breeze. Just after they left the lake the bear seemed to come out of nowhere. Though his father knew not to run from a bear, knew that there were better ways of taking care of the situation, such as throwing a rock into the bushes to cause a distraction or banging loud metallic objects together to create an obnoxious noise, the bear was too close. Dan said something like "Holy Shit!" after which Phillip and he ran like hell.

The bear was fast, and running was the wrong thing to do. Bears aren't hunters like mountain lions, but they will chase and batter if scared.

"Throw him the fish!" Dan yelled.

Phillip couldn't fathom throwing his fish away like that. He was proud of his catch. He couldn't wait for his mother to see that he had brought home dinner.

"Throw him the goddamn fish!" his father yelled again.

They were both running as fast as they could, listening to the stomping of weight as the bear tried to keep up with them.

"He's gaining on us, son, throw him the fish, *quick*!"

Phillip turned his head to see the snarling foaming mouth of the bear hulking after them, a massive shape of brown fur shifting this way and that. At that moment fear overwhelmed his pride and he threw the chain of fish back at the bear.

As Phillip turned his head back around to see where he was running, he caught his foot in between the branch of a fallen tree. His father yelled jump, but it was too late. Phillip's foot snapped, caught on the tree branch while gravity and momentum lunged the rest of his body forward over the fallen tree.

Fortunately the bear became preoccupied with the fish. Dan turned round for his son, keeping one eye on the brown monster that was ripping apart their dinner.

Phillip was screaming. "Shhhhhhhhhh!" his father cooed. "We've got to get out of here, and fast. When that bear's done with our fish he's gonna charge us again. You have to be brave, son, strong and tough." Phillip cried, his face streaming with tears. "I know your leg's hurt, probably broken, but we have to get outta here."

His father picked him up freeing his damaged leg from the twisted branches of the tree. "Put your arm around me, son," Dan said. "I can brace you, but you're gonna have to walk on your good foot, and fast. C'mon, son."

Dan and Phillip started walking away from the bear. Not fast, but it would have to do. Phillip whined and cried and tried to give up more than a few times. His father persisted and told him to be tough, to be brave.

It was this thought that made Phillip's sad mourning for his parents turn into angry rage. Tony had told him his father was an abusive drunk, but that wasn't true. If it hadn't been for his father he never would have made it out of the forest alive. He would have tripped over the log and been mauled there helpless to his injury.

"I have to be tough. I have to be brave."

Phil took the keys and began trying them in the cuff's lock. There was only one key on the ring that was small enough to fit and fit it did. Philip was free from the first obstacle, but what was next?

A weapon. He needed to arm himself. He was virtually defenseless against Tony's guns, but a knife would be better than nothing. Perhaps he could hide or sneak up on Tony unexpectedly.

Risking a peek outside, Phillip stood just slightly, hunched over so he could duck quickly if he were to see Tony. He could see nothing. He raised himself a bit more still seeing nothing until he was fully erect. Now he could see something. He could see Tony sprawled out on the driveway.

* * *

Outside, the air was still quite chilly as the sun was beginning to thaw the icicles hanging from the eaves. Not only did Phillip

122

dress for the cold, he equipped himself with several knives and an axe. He also took Tony's keys for good measure. During his panic of gathering warm clothes and weapons he tried to call the police, but the lines were still down, including the Internet.

He wasn't sure what to do. Was Tony dead? By the look of the bruising, the black eye and the bloody nose, he hoped so. It would save him the dirty choice of killing the man himself, and when it came right down to it, could he? Phillip wasn't sure he could. Murder may come natural to a freak like Tony, but for a child like Phillip it was incomprehensible.

Phillip stood at the edge of Tony's feet looking closely for the man's chest rising and falling. It was hard to see with so many layers of clothes, but he knew other ways to detect life in such temperatures. There were faint tendrils of steam shallowly rising with every breath, indicating that Tony was indeed still alive.

Phillip backed up as if Tony would rise at any moment. He could take the axe, chop Tony's head off and be done with it. It would be easy, but Philip wouldn't be able to live with himself.

He decided to carefully search Tony's jacket for his guns. If he could disarm the man, Phillip wouldn't be so damn vulnerable; he would be the one pointing the gun, making the demands. He would be in charge.

The idea of rummaging through a maniac's pockets while he was knocked out was crazy. It would be far too easy to wake the lunatic, and then what? A torture worse than his father's? Perhaps African sting bees and then a knife to cut the thickened, welted flesh off, followed by cutting off his eyelids forcing him to watch the sick bastard fornicate with his mother's corpse.

Phillip gasped. How could he think of something so vile?

After watching his parents brutally murdered, those kind of thoughts became ingrained in certain parts of his mind, branded there as a mental scar that would never fully heal.

Kneeling before his captor's body, Phillip carefully patted the jacket feeling for the lump of a gun. His examination was negative yet he knew the man must be armed, probably with both of his father's guns. He searched lower, watching Tony's face for any sign of consciousness, scaling his belt with delicate fingers until, on the right hand side, he felt the handle of the revolver.

Phillip moved Tony's jacket out of the way revealing the gun. For a moment, he looked at the weapon wondering if he should take it. His mind screamed 'yes, take the damn gun' while his conscience warned him away, telling him the removal of the gun would surely wake Tony. *Tony's a nasty old dog*, his conscience warned him, *and you should let sleeping dogs lie*.

His heart, on the other hand, was telling him to take the gun and point it at Tony if he were to wake. Point it at him and pull the trigger if necessary. This was the bastard that brutalized his family, after all, a rotten beast that deserved no less than death.

He went with his heart and pulled the revolver slowly from its confinement between Tony's belt and his waist. Though it was near freezing, sweat had beaded on Phillip's forehead, his nerves getting the better of him. At one point, the gun seemed to get caught, perhaps on Tony's belt. Phillip jiggled it slightly, breath held in anticipation of waking the sleeping monster, and it came loose sliding free, at which point a noise came from the road.

Phillip jerked his head up just in time to see the first of the snow plows barrel past the driveway throwing a wave of snow onto the hill opposite the house. The sound of the machine was deafening after such antagonizing silence. Phillip jumped backward losing his balance and landed on his rump. He held the gun firmly in his hand, lifting his head to see if Tony would awaken from his self-inflicted slumber.

After a moment, Phillip stood looking down on Tony, whose face hadn't changed. He was out cold, figuratively and literally.

Phillip wasn't sure what he should do. The snowplow would be coming back to plow the other side of the road and surely that would wake Tony. If only he could restrain Tony, tie him up or maybe . . .

Phillip felt the urge to run into the house but walked softly instead for fear of waking Tony.

He returned with the handcuffs. Though he would have liked to cuff Tony's hands behind his back—preferably with a rope tied around his neck that would dig into his flesh with his every move—he was unwilling and unable to move Tony's girth. Phillip slapped one cuff on Tony's right hand and then the other on his left, leaving him there on the cold ground with his hands neatly resting over his stomach like a corpse ready for burial.

Phillip wondered if the driver of the snowplow saw him and Tony. Probably not, and if he had, he probably would have thought nothing of it assuming that they were shoveling their driveway like so many others must be doing.

Tony was knocked out, maybe dying, and now that he was restrained there was no better time for Phil to start digging his way out. Tony's car was already free of snow; all Phillip had to do was finish digging his way to the street. He picked up the dented snow shovel and began the diligent backbreaking work of shoveling the driveway.

At ten, he had never driven a car. Some kids are given driving lessons on old back roads or in empty stadium parking lots, but SR 54 was no road for student drivers, especially ten year olds.

As Phillip shoveled the snow, he listened to the keys jingling in his pocket knowing they were the very keys to his destiny. What his destiny was he did not know. At this point it was to be free from Tony, but after that, he wasn't certain. Without parents to house, feed and raise him, where would he go? To a foster home? He sure hoped not. Maybe he could stay with his aunt Shelly. That would be a lot better than a stinking hell-house foster home.

The small boy who only a year ago outran a bear then limped home on a broken foot now stood in the driveway of a home he would never look at again, never regard as the warm, fuzzy place where he grew up. He shoveled snow to the left and to the right, blazing a path to SR 54, a road only half cleared by the snowplows. Behind him, lying on the paved driveway, was a vicious sociopath with one hell of a personality disorder; in the backyard were his parents in a shallow grave covered by several feet of snow.

Could it get any worse than this?

The keys in Philip's pocket made the noise not of a freedom bell, but a soft muffled freedom jingle. He listened to the jingle and it fueled him to work harder, to shovel faster. He kept his eye out for another plow, one that would shovel the snow from his side of SR 54. There was time. He had another half an hour of shoveling to clear a decent path for Tony's car. If the plow didn't make it back by then, Phillip would just have to shovel his way to the other side of the street himself.

Though the scene was grim and sad, though Phillip was going to have to look forward to a whole new life with excruciating circumstances, he could finally see freedom, hear it in his pocket. He had acquired the gun and wrangled the villain, and just as soon as he could clear the driveway, he could get away and call the police.

He almost felt safe for the first time in forty-eight hours, then he heard soft words from behind him.

" . . .Randy you s-s-son-of-a . . . "

Chapter 20
Freedom, maybe

The Madness! Phillip turned cautiously half thinking to drop the shovel and pull the revolver. *I didn't even check to see if it's loaded*, he scolded himself.

Tony was still on the ground, his head swaying slightly, mouth trying to form words.

"Randy, stop it!" Tony yelled suddenly.

Phillip decided to keep shoveling as fast as he could. If Tony were to wake he could very well make things difficult and the last thing Phillip wanted to do was to shoot a man, no matter how ugly the man's soul was.

Snow flew hither and thither with each swing of the shovel. Behind him Phil could hear a halfcocked argument between Tony and Randy as if they were fighting over who was in control of Tony's mind. In the distance, Phillip could hear a snowplow coming. He couldn't tell from which direction though. Probably it was coming down his side of the street.

"Hey!" Tony's voice yelled.

Phillip turned to see Tony cocking his head in his direction.

"What the fuck are you doing!"

Shoveling even faster, Phillip ignored Tony keeping a watchful eye on him with every shovel of the snow.

"Dammit, Randy, look what you did! The little shit has me handcuffed!"

* * *

Look at you, dude. You should have listened to me, Randy said to Tony in the private confines of his confused mind.

"You fucking shit-faced asshole, look what you've done to me! Look!" Tony wiggled trying to gain stance on the icy driveway.

You're wiggling around like a fuckin fish, Randy laughed hysterically at his brother's expense.

"Shut up!"

Phillip stopped shoveling momentarily with his hand hovering over the revolver tucked into his belt, ready to use it if he had to. Behind him, the snowplow passed once again on the opposite side of the road. Turning to see the plow pass by, Phillip cursed it.

On his knees, Tony reached to the left and then to the right of his waist. "He took my revolver!" He then tried to reach behind his back finding it impossible with the handcuffs on his wrists.

As Phillip watched, he saw what Tony was reaching for as his body became askew revealing his belt where the other gun was tucked away. Phil hadn't located that gun when he searched because Tony had been lying on his back.

"Shit!" Tony said, ignoring his brother's laughing insults.

Sitting on the ground, Tony stuck his foot through the loop of his handcuffed arms doing the trick in reverse that people did in the back of police cars to get their cuffed hands from behind their back and into a more comfortable position in front of them.

Phillip saw this for what it was and made a dash sliding toward his captor (now his captive) with the shovel above his head.

"No you don't," Phillip said bringing the shovel down on Tony's cranium, laying him out once again.

Phillip dropped the shovel taking a few steps backward, shocked at his actions. He hadn't used the gun, for which he was grateful, but knocking someone unconscious was a terrifying first for him.

"You have to be strong, you have to be tough," he reminded himself. Reaching cautiously, he pulled the gun from Tony's belt. He slid it under his belt on his left hip suddenly feeling like a gunslinger.

Grabbing the shovel, he returned to the edge of the driveway to clear away the remaining snow. Tony be damned, there was nothing he could do now. He was as defenseless as Phillip was when he woke up this morning.

* * *

Fifteen minutes later a decent path was cleared for Tony's car. Phillip would have felt better using one of his parent's cars, but would have to unbury the vehicle then search for the keys, and that could take half the day. The keys might even be buried with them in

128

the back yard. He shivered at the thought, and he wasn't about to dig up his parent's bodies.

Tony showed no sign of waking, slumped over in the same uncomfortable position with his cuffed hands between his legs.

Phillip tried the large key in the door; it opened to his slight dismay. He sat in the car feeling wholly out of place. Fortunately, he was tall for his age, which gave him an advantage at pushing the pedals while seeing above the dashboard. He stuck the key in the ignition and cranked it.

The motor turned but did not ignite. The car was cold. He tried again and heard the engine roar to life. Phillip didn't know cars very well, but he knew from past winters that it was good to let the engine run for a few minutes before putting the car into gear.

Phillip turned to look out of the rearview window for Tony to rise again. He hoped the man would stay down for just another minute or two so he could get the car onto SR 54. At the edge of the drive, a snowplow barreled past, finally on the right side of the road. Phillip wanted to smile but couldn't bring himself to do so.

"Better time than never," Phil said cranking the gear shifter into reverse.

Putting slight pressure on the gas pedal the car jerked backwards. Phillip hit the break surprised at how easily the car had glided backward. Letting his foot off the brake, he tried the gas a bit more cautiously, launching the car backwards, once again too fast.

Without breaking, Phillip turned the wheel. There was a crunch as he scraped against his fathers truck with the front bumper of Tony's car. Snow shook free and fell to the ground revealing the now scratched black paint of his father's truck. The damage didn't matter. The only thing that mattered was getting onto the highway and into town.

Phillip braked the car just before backing into a snow laced pine tree. Straight ahead was Tony lying on the frozen drive looking pathetic, like a second rate escape artist who couldn't get out of a simple pair of handcuffs. Phil had half a mind to put the car in drive and run the bastard over, but he resisted the brutal impulse, cranking the steering wheel to face the sloping driveway that led to his freedom.

A faint snow began to fall, nothing that would hold up, just a lingering reminder of the storm. Phillip cranked the gear shifter into drive, took one last look at Tony now speckled with tiny fragments

129

of ice that dissolved into his clothes as they landed on him, and gave the car some gas, lurching it forward with what seemed to Phillip as too much ease. He hit the brakes again stopping the vehicle abruptly in learning-to-drive fashion.

With another look to make sure Tony was still out, Phillip pressed his foot onto the gas pedal as softly as he could, feeling the engine come to life at his command. He strode up the driveway slowly, afraid that he may jettison out onto the highway and get into a wreck. This wasn't likely being that there hadn't been a car on the road except for the snowplows, but he feared it nonetheless.

"You come back here!" Tony's voice blasted from behind.

Phillip turned to look, taking his foot off the gas petal. Tony was attempting to stand, screaming and yelling. The car started to roll backward down the sloped driveway toward Tony. Phil panicked slamming his foot on the break causing the tires to catch the slippery asphalt sliding the car backward.

"Stop the car, it's gonna hit me! STOP!" screamed Tony.

Phillip let off the brake and hit the gas. The tires spun in place, fishtailing the rear end slightly.

Phillip, sweating and panicking, didn't know what to do. He had never even driven a car before, much less on an icy road. The brake made the car slide backward and the gas made it slide in place. He had to get the hell away from the house before Tony opened the door and pulled him out. Cuffed hands or not, Tony would be able to harm him.

He let his foot off the gas slowly to see what would happen and to his gleeful surprise, the car caught asphalt and glided up the driveway leaving Tony behind, sulking and screaming, thrashing around like a madman caught in some kind of mental loop.

Tony risked the highway without caution, turning the wheel to the right toward town. On his way out of the driveway he clipped a rather large mound of snow beneath which was the mailbox Tony had ran into when he decided to take refuge in what appeared to be a cozy looking house. Tony was incoming mail, a bad package; Phillip was outgoing mail, a good but slightly damaged package.

The road was shifty and slick, snow piled high on either side from the snowplows. In the center of the road, there was a white divider of snow that Phillip followed in order to keep himself on the right side of the road.

The car seemed to want to move on its own, sliding slightly

this way and that. For an experienced driver the sliding would have been easy to handle, but for ten-year-old Phillip, it was all he could do to keep the car straight.

He was getting a hold of the idea behind winter driving until he hit a patch of black ice.

Chapter 21
Black Ice

The car slid uncontrollably. Phillip, being a very inexperienced driver, slammed the brakes sending the vehicle further into a spin across the highway only to be stopped when the rear end slammed into a tree jolting Phillip into the steering wheel face first knocking him unconscious.

* * *

The second snowplow came upon the crashed car ten minutes after Phil lost control. The driver stopped the plow to check the car. The accident must have been recent since he hadn't heard anything on the CB from the plow driver that was ahead of him.

"What the . . . " the driver said at sight of the child hunched over the drivers seat.

He tapped the window with his knuckle alerting Phillip who woke sharply, scared that the rapping was that of Tony. Phillip looked at the man on the other side of the car and screamed and screamed.

In his mind there was a tickle, an irritating itch, like crawling bugs cooing to him, telling him to grab the gun.

The snowplow driver put his hands out, palms forward, motioning the boy that everything was all right, but Phillip screamed and yelled, convinced the man he was looking at was Tony, convinced Tony would bust the window, reach in, grab him and pull him out to torture him the way he had tortured his father.

"It's okay, son, I wont hurt you. What's your name?"

Phillip screamed. He could see a glint in the man's eyes that he could swear was The Madness. His own brain churned in a way his father never had a chance to prepare him for.

The snowplow driver tried the door handle but it was locked. He looked up just in time to see the kid pull a gun on him. That was the last thought that registered in his mind before a bullet shattered both the window and his brain.

Chapter 22
Randy and Tony

Tony fought his non-responsive body, writhing and thrashing around. It was no use; he was losing control. He let himself fall to the ground. As long as he lay there submissively, he wasn't fighting to be in control.

Slowly he tried to pull his leg to his chest and slide it beneath his cuffed hands to be in a more compromising position. His body allowed him to do this. More comfortable with his hands in front of him rather than between his legs, he stood again feeling the muscles in his body fighting to keep him down.

"What the fuck! What...? What is this?"

You're not going anywhere, Randy said simply.

"You can't stop me."

Watch me. You're gonna get what you deserve, man.

Tony tried to fight his revolting muscles and decided against it. "What do you mean?"

What, you think I'm stupid? You think I don't know what happened back in Ohio?

"What the hell are you talking about?"

An onlooker would have thought Tony was talking to invisible snowmen.

You set me up. My own brother set me up for a pay off.

Tony couldn't help but smile. How he was being haunted by his brother he did not know, but the bastard had his facts in order.

"So you know about that, huh? What was I supposed to do? You were gonna get us both killed. At least this way I saved my own ass."

At my expense! Man, you really let me down, stabbed me in the back with a freakin sword. So I set you up.

Tony was speechless.

You wouldn't have killed anyone had it not been for me, and I'm gonna hold you here until the police arrive and see what you did.

Tony tried once again to stand, feeling as if he were sub-merged in thick tar. His brother was holding him there, by thought, by spirit—by what, he didn't know.

* * *

The police arrived an hour later after taking care of the strange car accident/homicide a few miles up the highway. As the police drove up SR 54, they pulled into the first house that had a shoveled drive. That's where they found Tony.

The police car pulled into the driveway stopping several feet from Tony who was violently trembling and shaking.

"Is that Tony from the bank?" one officer said.

"Shit, I think it is."

Both police officers knew Tony from the bank, neither sus-pecting he would be as cold blooded as the boy in the car said he was.

"Is it the right guy, you think?"

"Has to be. It's just like the boy said, and it's the right ad-dress.

Both cops drew their pistols before exiting the car.

* * *

You finally made a mistake, and when she recognized you it freaked you out. You thought it would be so easy, such a well thought out plan, and without me there to fuck things up it would have gone smoothly.

Tony listened to his brother as he watched the cop car roll into the driveway. He recognized the police officers as regular pa-trons of the bank.

There's a shit-load of money in the trunk, isn't there? More than we ever scammed. How much do you think, half a mil? More?

Tony didn't respond for fear of looking crazier than he was. He wondered what was taking the cops so long.

The perfect crime, without me of course. Couldn't have pulled this one off had you not set me up back in Ohio to be shot up by the police. Now it's your turn.

What's taking them? Why don't they just come out here and get it over with, thought Tony, though he found it difficult to think for himself over Randy.

Clean out the bank just before a snowstorm. Must have taken you years to concoct that plan. Almost foolproof too, that is, if you had gotten home in time. After she recognized you I fed on your fears.

The doors opened, the police officers exiting cautiously, guns drawn.

I manipulated your mind, set a trap just like you did to me, and this is where you meet the same end, bro. This is where the cops shoot you.

"Put your hands where we can see them," one of the cops said.

Tony struggled to put his hands above his head but couldn't. Randy wouldn't let him.

"Put your hands in the air where we can see them!"

Tony tried to move, fought his brother's pull, and just as the third warning was being shouted at him, his body burst into animation—very threatening animation—as if he were going to attack the police.

Both cops fired their pistols unloading both clips into Tony out of sheer fear, laying him out on the pavement riddled with holes. Randy laughed as the cops shot Tony, laughed as he fell to the ground, and was laughing as he took his last breath.

Chapter 23
Phillip and the Money

The money was discovered later as investigators searched the vehicle. The mysterious robbery of the bank and the brutal killings off SR 54 were thought to be tied together, but until the money was found there was no proof other than Tony being the last one at the bank before the storm. The security tapes had been swiped.

Phillip was sent to a psychiatric hospital. It was never established just why he shot and killed the snowplow driver, though it was assumed that he was frightened and thought the man to be Tony.

Phillip hasn't been making much progress in his sessions, however. Now, at age fifteen, he has taken to a very unsettling hobby of drawing a series of comic books he calls "The Madness," which features extreme violence in the form of torture. These comic books alone are red flags against his replacement into society, though the artwork is quite phenomenal.

Phillip has also been known to give fellow psych patients nasty welts, what he likes to refer to as 'African sting bees.'

About the Authors

Craig Saunders lives in Norfolk, England with his wife and three children. He used to have three black cats but they were unlucky.

After an honours degree in Japanese and Law, Craig spent five years working in Japan, where he began writing fantasy and science fiction. His real passion, though, was always horror. His stories, spanning many genres, have featured in publications too numerous to count...but he still tries.

Scarecrow is Craig's first novella, and Rain, his debut novel, is out soon. Visit www.petrifiedtank.blogspot.com for news and updates.

Robert Essig began writing as a result of his fascination with everything horror—books, magazines, movies, etc. His work has been published in over 30 magazines and anthologies including Necrotic Tissue, Bards and Sages Quarterly, The Gloaming, and Tales of the Talisman. He is the editor of the anthologies Through the Eyes of the Undead (Library of the Living Dead), and Malicious Deviance (Library of Horror). His debut novel People of the Ethereal Realm is forthcoming from Twisted Library Press. Visit him at www.robertessig.blogspot.com.

Made in the USA
Charleston, SC
12 November 2011